AA

Aux Arc Novel

(Ozark Novel)

THE BOOK
OF JOHN

A NOVEL OF LOVE BY

ROBERT DEAN ANDERSON

ISBN 978-0-9720680-8-6

AUTHOR'S NOTE

The individual characters who appear in this book are wholly fictional. No character bears any resemblance to any person alive or dead whom I have ever known or met. Any apparent resemblance of a character to any person alive or dead is entirely coincidental.

For Great Granddaughter Natalie Wood who knows the

meaning of Love and always will.

1

BOONE QUIETLY swung the massive, oaken door open and stepped into the cathedral presence. A glow from the altar at the front illuminated the interior. The baby he carried lay sleeping in folded blankets. Blankets days past their due washing. Gently, even tenderly, he laid the baby on the planked floor just inside the doorway. Empty pews flanked the length of the center aisle. An aura existed here that did not exist outside. An aura too unusual to identify. The oaken door marked the edge of the outside world. Breathing became easier. A weight on the mind lifted, but a sorrow still lay in the heart.

Beside the baby he placed the small canvas bag of bottles, diapers and one can of formula. He halted, waiting, still and unmoving on both knees, trying to decide if a prayer should be recited. Did he even know a prayer? Finally with eyes closed, head bowed, he whispered, "Please, God, keep him safe," and leaned over to kiss the sleeping baby then left the church, closing the door softly.

The wispy light of morning sun spread along the horizon leisurely crossing the river at its own speed. The capital dome shown brilliantly from the gleam of early light. Along Jefferson Street toward the river stood the Amtrak station. A light glowed inside the station, but the door was locked. Boone sat on the curb in front of the old limestone building that made up Jefferson Landing now used by Amtrak. Hugging himself against the chill he wondered if the baby would stay warm. Thoughts of all the recent events played in his mind. Thoughts that always narrowed and returned to the baby.

Out of money, out of hope and out of friends he hung his head against his knees, his heart pounding in his chest. He could not hold back the tears.

AS DAYLIGHT expanded across the waking city, Boone opened the same front door of the same church. Traffic moved on the street behind him. Inside, the baby still bundled in blankets slept on the floor. The pews sat vacant, no one visible inside the church. He leaned over the baby and listened to his even breathing. The eyes opened and the blue in them revealed a brilliance as they focused and the soft, pink skin around them glowed. One isolated ray of sunlight broke through a leaded glass window and splashed a golden radiance onto the baby's face. Was that a smile there? Boone touched his hand to the baby's cheek and felt the warmth and miracle of life. He was so small, his entire head not much larger than the softball Boone pitched at school.

He placed the baby in his arms again, picked up the canvas bag and raised to go. A man stood there, dressed in a wrinkled sweat suit. He looked at Boone, at the baby.

"Do you need help?" the man asked, his voice friendly but firm.

Boone shrugged. "I wanted him to know God."

"I'm Father Pierce," the man said.

"T-T-Tom," Boone stuttered.

"I haven't seen you here before, Tom," the priest said.

"No, no. I haven't been here before."

"Would you like to have some hot chocolate? Some bacon and eggs maybe?" the priest asked.

Food sounded good. The baby began to squirm and made a mewing sound. "I'm supposed to watch him today. I guess I'd better get back."

"You live here then?"

Boone hesitated. "I'm staying here." Then added, "With my uncle."

The baby began to cry. Father Pierce took Boone by the arm.

"Come on, let's get some breakfast and feed this child. I think he's hungry. It is a boy, isn't it? Your cousin?"

Boone nodded. He walked beside the priest who still held Boone's arm, urging him toward the altar and the rear of the church. As they walked through that place where people aren't supposed to lie, Boone's face burned. They entered a small living quarters. A sofa, a chair, pictures on the wall, not much else. The corner of the room served as an abbreviated kitchen with a round table and two straight chairs. The priest opened the single door of a very small refrigerator and took out a plastic milk jug, removed a silver pan from inside one of the cabinet doors and poured milk into the pan. He sat the pan on one of two burners on a stove and turned a knob.

"If you'll hand me a bottle," he said to Boone, "we can heat up what that young man wants. Some food."

Boone sat in the upholstered chair and held the baby on his lap. He opened the canvas bag, took out a baby bottle, fished around inside the bag and brought out the can of formula.

The priest watched. "You seem to know how to take care of your cousin."

Boone held out the can and bottle to Father Pierce, the baby in his other arm. "Just open the can and pour it in the bottle."

"Does it need to be heated?"

"Uh, no."

The priest fixed the bottle as instructed and handed it back without heating it. "What's his name? Your cousin. His name isn't Tom also is it?" He was smiling as he said it.

"No."

The priest opened the small refrigerator again, took out a carton of eggs and a package of bacon. "How do you like your eggs, Tom. Over easy, no runny yolk? How?"

"I guess I'd like them cooked pretty solid."

"Two be enough or you think you could handle three eggs?"

"Well, maybe three eggs scrambled would be all right."

The priest placed long strips of bacon in a large black frying pan. "You need to call anyone at your uncle's house? Let them know the two of you are all right?"

"Uh, no."

"You do this often? Baby sit your cousin."

Boone never looked up. "Yes, quite a bit."

After turning the bacon, Father Pierce said, "There's a baby missing from the town of Eldon. You're not from Eldon are you?"

Before he answered, Boone adjusted the baby's position again. "I was thinking I already told you, we're from here."

"What's your uncle's name? Perhaps I know him."

Boone took the bottle from the baby who continued to suck with the nipple removed from his mouth.

"I think he needs to be changed," Boone said.

"Sure, go ahead." The bacon was placed on a plate and the priest began breaking eggs into the black skillet.

Boone ran his hand around inside the canvas bag and came out with a diaper. The priest looked at the diaper as Boone tried to hide the inside that was stained with urine. He placed the baby on the chair and changed the wet diaper for the dry one. The baby grasped the air with both hands, looking for the bottle, his face screwed into a grimace as if a vocal objection was about to be launched. When Boone gave the bottle to him again, the baby began sucking vigorously on the nipple.

"Bacon and eggs will be ready as soon as the toast is done," Father Pierce said. He placed two plates and utensils on the small round table. "What is your uncle's name?" he asked again.

Boone said, "They won't get into trouble will they? I mean, because I'm taking care of him. Because I'm . . . so young?"

"Priests' mission is to help people in trouble, Tom." He placed the bowl of scrambled eggs, the plate of bacon with two slices of toast on the table. He indicated with a wave of his hand that Boone should sit in one of the straight chairs. When they were both seated at the table, with the baby still working on the bottle as he curled up in one of Boone's arms, Father Pierce looked across at Boone, looked into his eyes directly and said, "It's people who get people into trouble, Tom."

THE BABY was asleep again, this time on the sofa. Boone held the cup of hot chocolate in both hands. The meal had been consumed in silence. He drank the rest of the hot chocolate and rose from the straight chair.

"I guess I better be going," he said. "Thank you for the eggs and bacon. And the hot chocolate."

"My good fortune," Father Pierce said. "Usually I have breakfast alone. It was a pleasure having you and your cousin at my table. Could I get anything else for you?"

"No. No thanks. I enjoyed the meal. I mean, it was good."

"Anytime you'd like to have breakfast with me, the invitation is open. Will you be showing up in church for mass?"

Boone busied himself with the canvas bag. He looked up. "We're not Catholic, Father."

"I gathered that. But we're all God's children, Tom. It looks like you need some more diapers for your cousin. Do you need more of his formula?"

"I don't have any money, Father."

"And your uncle?"

Boone shook his head.

"What does your uncle and his family do, Tom? Are they

working today? There is someone at their house isn't there?"

Boone slung the straps to the canvas bag over his shoulder and picked the baby up from the sofa. "I best be going, Father."

Father Pierce went to a small chest sitting close to the sofa and pulled a drawer out. He took something from the drawer and handed Boone some bills. Boone looked at the money.

"I wouldn't be able to pay you back, Father."

"It's not a loan, Tom. It's not a gift. It's care for one of God's children."

Boone shoved the money in his pocket. He started for the door.

"I have the feeling you came here for help, Tom," Father Pierce said. "For something more than food or money."

Boone opened the door leading from the priest's living quarters, his back still to Father Pierce.

"You've given me more than I asked for, Father."

"If you have a problem, Tom, you don't have to bear it by yourself. There are people who can help. I can help."

"No, no one can help."

"Let's put that to test and see."

"I can't have the police involved, Father. If I told you about my life, you would have to call the police. People would be hurt."

"No, I don't call the police, Tom. It stays between the two of us. And with God. You haven't hurt someone have you?"

"No, no one has been hurt. The problems . . . the problems are between us, me and them. And can't anyone help."

When he turned to look at the priest, tears rimmed his eyes and ran down his cheek. "You're a good man, Father. A kind man. We thank you for that."

Before Father Pierce could say more, Boone and the baby were gone into the early morning where others with problems were preparing to take them into the world. Few out there could say they were without a problem of some kind.

2

ON A DAY one year earlier, Jack Blakely rose at dawn
with the rain falling. A rain that continued intermittently
throughout the day. He reported to his job site, sat in his
eight-year-old Ford pickup drinking bitter coffee from his
stainless steel thermos, wishing for a different drink. One he
rationed now. He got out during a short break in the weather
to begin rough-troweling the fresh concrete, but the concrete
trucks never came back. Somewhere around five, Jack and
the rest of the crew called it quits and left the site, some
headed towards the Construction Site Pub while a few, like
Jack, headed home.

Twila was there. Jack closed the door of the truck, raking
the air with it's metal-on-metal sound until he slammed it
hard to secure the latch. He swore silently to himself, noting
that the rain had at last stopped and the sun broke through
the gray dome overhead. He was a tall man with sharp, hard
features. Twenty years ago those features had been called
handsome by almost every young woman in Eldon. Today,
deep crevices from sun and exposure—plus the cigarettes
and the whiskey—spread like lines on a map, the ground-in
residue from Portland cement powder that was never coming

out of the pits and streaks within those crevices. All covered by three days of stubble that Jack had spotted gray in just this morning. And him only forty.

The rented house, a simple 25 by 40 ranch style had been added onto several times. The back door squalled almost as loud as the pickup truck's door when he opened it, bringing a call from Twila from the kitchen. He walked through the utility room, gave his work boots a cursory brush across the mat into the kitchen, just to keep Twila from griping about the grit he tracked in and wishing again he would take his boots off and leave them in the utility room, but Jack had a thing about walking around without shoes on. She stood at the counter mixing something in a bowl. He looked for and didn't see a drinking glass close to her hand.

Without looking up she said, "No work today, huh?"

He took off his hat and laid it on the table and took a seat there.

"Coffee?" she asked.

"Whiskey."

She glanced at him. Sharply. She hadn't seen him drinking whiskey for nearly a month now.

"You might want to have one yourself," he said. She stared at him.

"What happened?" she asked. She didn't move toward the cabinet where he kept his bottle of Old Granddad. He waited, as did she, and finally he got out of his chair and went to the cabinet, got the bottle, took two glasses from the shelf below and poured an abundant shot into each glass and held one out for her. She stared at it, continuing to mix the ingredients in the bowl.

"The deacon came to see me today," he said.

She stopped the mixing, the spoon halted in midair. "Frank Griffin?"

"Yep."

She went to the old style refrigerator with the freezer on top and opened it, brought out a tray of ice, popped two cubes from it and dropped them in one of the glasses of whiskey. She held the glass, waiting, watching him. He ignored the tray of ice she had set on the counter and took the other glass in his hand, then drank it all, set it back on the counter and poured another shot in it.

"The deacon's got a problem," he said.

"At the church?"

"At home."

"What do we have to do with the deacon's problem at home?"

"Boone."

"Boone? Our son?". She was concerned all right, he could see it in her face. Fifteen years and he knew the face, could read it like a billboard, could tell her inner-most feelings from the way her features were aligned. He didn't need to wait for her to ask more, but he waited anyway.

"What about Boone? How's he get involved with Frank Griffin's home life?"

"The deacon's daughter, Penny. She's pregnant."

Her face was unmoved for a moment, then it soaked in. Her hand went to her mouth and the eyes grew round. "Boone? He's saying Boone . . .? But how could he . . .? Boone? He just turned sixteen. How could he?"

Jack let it lay there for her to think about.

"He couldn't could he? I mean, sixteen? Could he do it at sixteen? I mean . . . does it come together, can he, do boys, I mean . . . sixteen? Could you do it at sixteen? I mean, you weren't sixteen when we, that is, you were what, twenty something. Boys at sixteen. Can they?"

"Well, he's starting to grow a beard," Jack said. "I guess puberty is past."

"But Boone . . ." She moved her hand away from her mouth and shook her head. "Boone wouldn't do that. Not Boone. He doesn't even date girls. Especially Penny Griffin. She's . . . what? A cheerleader? She runs with all those football players. Boone doesn't go around with that crowd."

"The deacon thinks he does, I guess."

"What are we going to do? I mean . . . what does Frank Griffin want us to do? Why does he come to see you?"

"He wants to know what we're going to do about it. Wants us to do the Christian thing, of course."

"What makes him think it was Boone? Boone just barely knows that girl. She's not in his class. I think she's a senior. Why Boone? Why doesn't he think it was one of those football boys?"

"Well, it seems Penny told him it was Boone."

"How far along is she?"

"About twelve weeks according to the deacon. Morning sickness and all. Took her to see old Doc Carlyle and he told them she was pregnant. So the deacon sat her down and had her come to Jesus or whatever it is he does, and she confessed her and Boone tussled around in the backseat of her fancy car and she came away—let's see, how did the deacon put it—tarnished and defaced with the terrible shame of being unmarried and with child. He implied it was all without Penny's consent."

"He's accusing our son of raping his daughter?"

"Well, he's not ready to go to the law about it. Not yet, anyway. He's feeling us out first, I guess. See what we're going to do about it. He's a little bit of— how is it they say on those TV shows?—in denial?"

She was silent, looking at the drink in her hands as if the answer to the problem might be there. Fifteen years ago it had been there, in the glass, in the bottle. But now? Her hands were still dusted with the mix she had been stirring and he noticed how those hands had aged. It came to him then like a revelation how much Twila had changed from that moment so long ago when she had come to him and told him she was pregnant with Boone. My God, his own son falling into the same trap he had, only the son was only sixteen, not twenty-five.

"We have to talk with him," Twila said without looking up. Dark rims lay under her eyes. Had they just now appeared or had he not taken note of them? Had he become indifferent to how she looked, only aware of how she nagged and gossiped and complained.

"We have to talk with Boone," she said again.

He agreed with a nod and had another drink from the bottle. The taste was acrid now, bitter, and he shoved the bottle away from him. Life goes along, one monotonous day after another until one day it takes a sharp right turn and you're headed into unknown territory. On that day you miss the routine of one monotonous day after another. You want your old life back, but you realize with a pang in your gut that it's gone. That things are never going to be the same again.

"Is he home?"

She nodded.

"Call him."

She looked at him, a firmness in her jawline that hadn't been there before. "I think it would be better if you did it."

He thought about it. He looked at the bottle, but it was uninviting. No help there. His own father had found all his answers inside a bottle and that's why he ended up in a grave at forty-five, a deadly knife slash on his throat. He'd bullied everyone, especially his own family, until, one night in a bar-room, he'd bullied one man too many and Jack had been left homeless after his mother packed her bags two weeks later and left Jack and two sisters to fend for themselves.

He got out of the chair and walked into the hallway. From the kitchen, Twila said, "Don't be mean, Jack. He's still only a boy."

"No," Jack said, "He's a man, now."

JACK HAD never understood his son. Though he looked in the face of his son and at his growing body and felt a relationship through that appearance, the inner boy was more like Twila. Playing ball in the backyard and on the Little League fields, he saw an athleticism much like his own. But Boone never pushed his skills. Never rejoiced in a home run or a throwout at the plate the way Jack did. Boone wasn't sharp in his schoolwork. Teachers said he had some kind of disorder. A-D-D they called it. He was supposed to take some pills that cost too damn much and Jack wasn't sure Boone even took the pills. Twila worked with him in his younger years, but many times Jack noticed the vacant look on Boone's face while Twila was laboring over a school report due the next day.

Boone liked to draw and diddle with pencils and paper. But that was just a phase. Once, while both were watching a St. Louis Cardinals' game on television, Jack noticed Boone scribbling on paper. He sneaked a look, expecting a sketch of perhaps Pujols slamming a home run or maybe a Carpenter strikeout. What he saw was a chipmunk on a skateboard.

Skateboarding had been another phase. Jack watched him in the street with a gang of other boys and Boone was clearly beyond the others in skill, but it was soon dropped in favor of BMX racing. His latest: he wanted a motorcycle. What he called a dirt bike. Jack was still looking for a way to connect with Boone, but when he got interested in Boone's newest interest, Boone had switched to something else. Apparently, his latest was girls.

He knocked on Boone's closed door and said, "Boone, you got a minute?"

A half minute later Boone's voice came through the door, "Yeah, come on in."

He found Boone poring over a stack of motorcycle magazines. Not *Playboys*, at least. He pulled a stool away from a piled up desk and sat. Boone looked up from the magazine, but kept his finger on the page.

Jack got right to it. "Frank Griffin came to see me today."

He saw the color change in Boone's face and the son dropped his eyes back to the magazine. Jack decided to wait for him, but Boone didn't say anything.

"He says you got his daughter Penny pregnant."

Boone's body quivered as if a sudden chill had hit him. He didn't look up.

"Anything to it?" Jack tried to keep his voice even, but it came out harsh and accusing. Boone looked out the window, avoiding Jack's eyes.

"I didn't know she was pregnant," he said, his words so low Jack wasn't sure what he had said until he ran them through his mind again.

Boone shook his whole body and his head went from side to side. "God, I never meant that. Why that? Why me?"

"What happened?" Jack asked.

Boone said a lot of gibberish, none of it making any sense. Finally, "She goes around with Duke Mansfield. You know, he's the big football star of the team. It was that night of the Turkey Day festival. We were all out in the street, it was getting dark, they turned on the lights and the cops kept telling us to go home, get off the street. I was with Dewey Dower and some others, just standing around. Here comes Duke and his gang, strutting down the street. All the girls with them giggling. Pukesville. Duke, he's telling everyone about Penny's bush." He looked at Jack.

"Yeah, I know what a girl's bush is."

"Saying things like, 'I've seen it, but she ain't let me in it, not till tonight.' Then Penny slaps him on the arm and he goes, 'Well, if I ain't there tonight, there's always Marsha Tackett.'"

He looked at Jack again, but Jack didn't have anything to say about that.

"Well, I'm probably the only boy in school who hasn't been with Marsha Tackett. Even Dewey has, so he says. And Penny says 'Go ahead. But don't come crawling back to me.' And with that Duke gets mean and they get in a pretty hot argument and Duke ends up slapping her face. Everybody just stood there while Penny's crying and I thought maybe the cops would come back and stop him, but he grabs Penny by one of her breasts and he begins to hurt her while he's telling her not to ever sass him back. And nobody is doing anything so I went over and told Duke maybe he better leave Penny alone. That's when he starts on me and tells me he's going to whip my ass and all that macho talk. The cops showed up about that time and I don't remember what else happened after that, except there I was with just me and Dewey and Penny standing there in the street. And she's crying and Dewey, he's no help. She tells me how thankful she is that I stopped Duke and could she drive me home and all, but she told Dewey he better walk home."

Jack said, "In her own car?"

Boone took out a handkerchief and blew his nose. Jack saw tears in the boy's eyes.

"Well, the Griffins are rich, I guess. She's older than me, a senior. She always has nice clothes and all and you know the house they live in."

Jack nodded. "He's the owner of All Right Construction, you know. The company I work for. He can afford to buy his daughter a car." But I can't afford a motorcycle for my son, Jack thought. Probably what Boone was thinking, too.

Boone closed the magazine, but continued looking at the front where a cyclist was flying through the air on the back of a shiny motorcycle. "Anyway," he finally continued, "We're in her car, but instead of driving me home we drove way out in the country ending up in the parking lot of the Mennonite church. She says something like, 'That sonofabitch,' and she began taking off all her clothes. I'm scared and nervous. She starts kissing me and rubbing my hands on her and . . . we ended up doing it."

Boone continued looking at the magazine. Jack thought about what to say. What was it he had said to Twila when she told him she was pregnant? He said, "That was about 12 weeks ago. That's what the doctor said. She's twelve weeks pregnant."

Nothing was said for a minute or two. Jack asked, "You think it's your baby?"

Boone shrugged. After a pause he said, "I told her it was the first time I'd ever done it and she said it was for her, too. But I kind of didn't think so."

"Why's that?"

Boone shrugged again, still looking away. "Well, Dewey, he thinks he knows all about everything. He says girls bleed a lot their first time."

Another pause and he said, "She knew how to do it. I didn't know anything. She laughed at me."

"What are you going to do about it?" Jack asked.

Boone looked at him, both fear and pleading in his eyes. "I don't know. I'm only sixteen."

"You're a man now," Jack said. "You took on a man's role so now you have a man's responsibility. Your life just took a new path. Nothing will ever be the same for you again. Growing up is over. Think about it. Go talk with the girl."

He got up to leave.

"We'll talk again."

3

BOONE HAD never seen a man with a metal leg before. Not in person, at least. Maybe on television when they were showing soldiers back from Afghanistan or Iraq after being injured from what they called an IED. The man was unshaven and his clothes, looking like army fatigues Boone had seen in the Army/Navy surplus store, appeared to have not been removed for washing or sleep for weeks. Boone had supposed the spot under the bridge uninhabited and had decided on the spot for himself and the baby to spend the night. Now, with just enough light to make out the stumbling soldier–Boone assumed the man was a soldier—Boone grew afraid, not for himself, but his first thought was what the man might do to the baby.

He gathered the baby up in his arms and taking the canvas bag, made ready to flee as fast as he could. How fast could he run with the baby? Surely fast enough to get away from a man with a metal leg, though scenes from a YouTube selection of a man with such a leg winning a race flashed through his thoughts.

The man saw them and stopped. Boone gaged which

direction would make for the fastest escape. The man grunted. "Sorry, M'am. I didn't mean you any harm. I didn't see you there."

Boone kept his silence.

"I'll move along, I won't disturb you any."

He stood looking at Boone, a rolled up sleeping bag under one arm, the other hand holding a red plastic basket like the ones in Target that you carried your purchases in. It was piled to overflowing.

"You all right, M'am?" the man said, his voice soft. "You need help?"

Boone shook his head. The baby squirmed in his arm and the man looked at the moving bundle.

"You fixing to sleep here, under the bridge, with your baby?"

Boone did not respond.

"I've been staying here for about a month, now," the man said, conversationally as if talking to a friend. "It's pretty safe. Some others come once in a while, but not often." He pointed overhead where the sound of traffic on the bridge created an overtone. "Kinda noisy. Most people like us go out to the park. You just have to move when you see the police coming. This is the state capital, you know. They don't like folks like us sleeping in their nice manicured parks."

Boone watched, squeezing the bundle and the baby. If the man made a move towards them, Boone would run where some waist-high brush grew. Tougher for a man with a metal leg to follow. The man mistook him, with the day's light nearly gone, for a girl or a woman because of the baby.

"If it would make you feel better, I'll go on out to the park," the man said. "I came here to be by myself. I don't hurt people anymore. I did that for a while and look where it got me." He pointed to his metal leg.

Boone said, "I don't want any trouble. I just want people to leave me and my baby alone."

"Are you a boy?" Slightly incredulous.

"The baby's my son," Boone said. He moved two steps toward the high weeds. The man didn't move.

"I'll be damned," the man said. "You don't sound like you're old enough to have a . . .how old are you?"

"Old enough."

"Look," the man dropped his sleeping bag on the ground. "I ain't going to hurt nobody. You seen what I seen then you'd know. You'd be like me. They tell me at the VA I'm just suffering from some kind of post traumatic stress disorder. PTSD they called it. Just takes time, they said. You'll be all right. Well, I ain't all right. I saw babies no bigger than that one blown to pieces. Body parts flying through the air hitting you in the face. You know how it feels to have somebody's guts—some little kid's guts—splattered all over you?"

He paused, looked away and said barely audible, "No, of course you don't."

The man hung his head and dropped the basket on the ground. Items spilled out, cans of food, bottles of what Boone thought looked like the wine his dad bought.

"I seen the inside of hell," the man said. "Don't ever go there. You never get away."

The man's voice was breaking and in the scant amount

of light under the bridge, reflections of tears were visible on the man's face.

"You don't have to go," Boone surprised himself by saying. "I have to protect the baby."

"Well," the man said, wiping an arm across his face. Gruffer now: "I like company, but mostly people don't want me around. I get to jabbering about what I've seen and most folks don't want to hear that. Guys come back in one piece, people are all over them. 'Oh, thank you for protecting us. What can we do for you?' Well, I say, can you erase what's inside my head? Can you make me whole again. Can you fix it so I'm not a cripple, so people don't look at me like that again?"

He half turned away from Boone. "No, of course you can't."

He bent to retrieve the items spilled from his basket. "I won't bother you none, I promise. I love babies. Last thing in the world I'd do now is hurt a baby."

He stood, holding the basket and the sleeping bag back under his arm. "You hadn't ought to be here, you know. Not good for a baby. But, they're tough, babies are. You should see what some of them have to put up with over there."

After a pause, he said, "No, nobody should have to see that. Listen, I'm going to sleep over here," pointing, "I won't be noisy or bother either of you none. I think you need help. I wish I could help you. Trouble is, I can't even help myself."

"I just don't want anybody to hurt the baby," Boone said.

"What happened to the baby's momma?" the man asked. "Or, maybe you'd rather not say. Don't matter."

"She wanted an abortion, but her parents wouldn't let her. Something about God not killing babies. They told her she had to give the baby away. Nobody asked me. They took a DNA and the baby's mine. My parents, well, the state wouldn't let them adopt him, my dad has a record and my mom drinks a lot, but the mother was the one decided. Or rather, it was her parents. Her dad's a deacon in the Baptist church. He knows the judge. The judge gave the baby to somebody in Iowa. He's my son, not theirs. She doesn't want my son, then I'll take him."

Boone waited, relieved that he finally got to tell somebody, even a man with a metal leg, but he was surprised about babbling on that way.

"So, *I* took him," Boone said. The baby was sound asleep now, so Boone knelt and laid him softly on the ground. He began gathering leaves for a bed. He had stopped watching the man now and felt stronger than he had when the man first appeared and decided he could protect the baby if he had to.

"So, they're looking for you," the man said.

"Probably."

"They have an Amber Alert out for the baby?"

"No, her father wouldn't want them to do that. Too much publicity and everyone would be talking about him and his illegitimate grandson."

"Okay, why don't we try and get you on the train tomorrow. Get you away from here."

Boone looked up. "How am I going to do that?"

The man spread his sleeping bag on the ground. He straightened, "I'm Roger," he said. "I'll think of some way.

I've been living with the impossible. You had anything to eat?"

"I'm okay," Boone said. "My name's . . .Boone . . ." not intending to give his real name, it just popped out.

The man looked at the baby. "What's his name?"

Boone was stumped, realizing he hadn't given it any thought. "I . . .I don't know yet."

"Boone junior," the man said. He sat on the sleeping bag and unbuckled the straps around his truncated leg then held it up. "See my souvenir from the Middle East? Didn't cost me a dime. All aluminum, only weighs a few pounds. The government's gift to me for getting shot at and blown up. The penalty is having to wear the damn thing. My punishment for not dying. Cheaper for the government if I just died."

The bitterness that had popped into the man's voice just as quickly disappeared. "I've got some money I was saving for another bottle or two of wine, but tomorrow, instead, what say we go to McDonald's and have breakfast?"

"Uh, yeah, sure. But, I've got some money."

"No, you two are my new friends. I insist. Nothing but the best for my friends. Egg McMuffins all around. Except for Boone junior, of course. Maybe one of those Mango Pineapple Smoothies for him."

The man laughed and for the first time since kidnapping his son Boone laughed too. "Don't want him spitting up on me."

Roger stretched out on his bed, arms locked behind his head. "Gets pretty noisy overhead about six o'clock in the morning. Better get some sleep while it's quieter."

A boat chugged along on the river yards away from their spot under the bridge. A spotlight on the boat played along each bank, back and forth.

"If we were pirates," Roger said, "we'd capture that boat and go all the way to New Orleans."

Boone fixed the baby's bed and laid him and the blankets on it. He stretched out the black sheet of plastic beside the baby and lay down. Directly overhead ran the steel and concrete construction, but toward the horizon stars were visible.

"I think I'll name him John," Boone said, looking and talking to the stars. "My dad's name is John, but everyone calls him Jack. John's a good name. Lots of important men named John. And my John's going to be an important man someday."

Roger snored, traffic overhead buzzed and rumbled, the boat's horn sounded from out on the river and the baby just now named John made a sucking sound. And, once again, Boone silently cried himself to sleep.

4

THE NOISE proved not to be as bad as the dust and sediment that sifted through the bridge overhead. Boone woke early, before the sun broke the horizon, and felt the grit on his face. He reached for the baby, pulled back a fold in the blanket and wiped at the baby's face. At first, he feared the baby wasn't breathing, but felt the pulse under the dress-like smock and knew relief.

The baby stirred, his unfocused eyes roaming until they settled on Boone bending closer. Boone dipped into the canvas bag, searching for an unopened can of formula, found it, opened it, felt the plastic bag of formula inside, and began feeding the baby.

"Come on, John," he said, trying out the name he had given the baby. The baby searched eagerly for its nourishment, found it and replaced the agitated mewing sound with a sucking noise.

"You know you're going to have to find a better place for that baby," Roger said, standing over them. Boone hadn't heard him come up to them and that worried him.

"I know," Boone said, holding the bottle while the baby worked on it. "I can't decide what to do."

Roger, leaning on a telescoping metal cane, holding his unattached metal leg said, "Right now, I'm going to go get a shower, clean up, change clothes. You can, too, if you want. Then we're going after those Egg McMuffins."

"We're going to a house?"

"No, well, it's as good as a house. I can get you in, too. Try not to show off the baby too much."

"Is it safe?"

"Worst they could do is run us off. I'll have to make up a story if anyone sees us. People get suspicious, you know how that is. Especially they see the baby."

"I don't know," Boone said. He watched the baby feed himself and felt of the soggy diaper. "I have to protect him. The police see him and he'll end up in Iowa."

He choked back the strong feeling he always felt when thinking of the baby in Iowa. "He's my son," he blurted out. "If I'm old enough to be a father then I have to take care of him."

"I'm on your side," Roger said. "Listen, why don't we put him in my basket, people won't notice him. We get over to the place I'm going before people get out so much, we get cleaned up and over to McDonalds and we're just normal people."

"I don't feel normal anymore," Boone said. He pulled a clean-up paper cloth out of the pop-up container and wiped the dribbling formula off the baby's chin. "Me and John, we won't ever be normal again."

THE SIDEWALK ran alongside the river, then without signs or notices became a rock strewn path. Roger carried the basket with Baby John inside and even with his aluminum, high tech leg, Boone had to walk quickly to maintain his pace. Between the back side of several metal warehouse type buildings bordering the pathway—now not much more than a trail through tall weeds—a collection of scrap, junk and debris lay scattered. Roger halted behind the third building, an older, and larger one than the others, and he held the basket out to Boone.

"This is it," he said. "I've got a key to the back door. We go through there, down a hallway to a restroom that has a couple of shower stalls in it. People only use the showers after work, not before. If anybody comes in, just ignore them. Act like you belong there. Grab some paper towels and get inside one of the shower stalls."

"What about John?" Boone asked. "What if he starts crying?"

"Let me handle it. I'll be in the shower stall next to you. If I hear him, I'll come out and take care of anyone happens to be in there."

"What if we get caught?"

Roger waved a hand. "Stop worrying, will you? I got us covered."

A patch of weeds and a pile of broken concrete blocks led to the back door of the building. Roger fished through a collection of items in one of his pockets and selected a key. The door made a screeching sound when it opened. Inside an empty hallway, barely light enough to make out the doors on either side, ran the length of the building.

"Come on," he said and moved quickly along the hall until he came to a door that had RESTROOM printed on it. Boone held the basket and his bag of baby items and clothes close to his chest. Roger opened the door and flipped on the light switch inside. A bare concrete floor led to several stalls around toilet stools running along the back wall with shower stalls in the corner. The dingy room smelled musty like a high school locker room. Roger, already pulling paper towels out of a metal dispenser on the wall, indicated Boone should do the same, then he filled a cupped hand full of liquid soap from a dispenser over a hand sink. Boone had trouble accomplishing the same with the baby's basket and his loaded bag. By the time he was finished, Roger was already in one of the shower stalls. Boone found a bench in the other one and set Baby John in the red basket on the bench. He pulled the blanket aside to check on the baby and saw those brilliant, blue eyes staring at him.

Water ran in Roger's shower before Boone undressed and entered the enclosure. The spray from the shower head turned hot and Boone adjusted the temperature, lathered and rinsed quickly, then stood under the spray enjoying his first shower in days. On a whim, he pushed the rubber curtain aside, went to the basket where Baby John still stared at him, and undressed the baby. He took him in his arms and went back under the spray and when the soft, warm water hit the baby, his face puckered up and he started crying. Not loudly, but enough to worry Boone. He found another soap dispenser on the shower wall and lathered the baby, rubbing his hand over the soft, warm body.

"What's going on in there?" from Roger.

"It's John, he loves it," Boone called back, laughing as he did. He began talking to the baby who still had his face puckered for another cry, but soon his face relaxed and with the flow of the warm water, Boone felt the baby's stiffened muscles loosen. He moved the baby's head under the water and Baby John closed his eyes tightly and clenched his mouth, When his head was lifted out of the direct spray of warm water, a smile appeared on his mouth.

Roger was out of the shower stall when Boone heard the door to the restroom open. Boone heard a man say, "Roger, that you in there?"

"Yeah," Roger answered. His aluminum foot clanked against the concrete floor.

"Dammit, Roger, I already told you not to come sneaking in here using our restroom. How the hell you getting in here? You got a key?"

"You're lucky I come in here, Garrett," Roger was saying. "I cleaned all that black mold out of your shower. Damn, don't you boys ever clean things up?"

"Who's in here with you?" the man Roger had called Garrett asked. "Who's in that other shower?"

"A friend, Garrett. I told him it would be all right."

"No, dammit Roger, it's not all right. It's not all right for you to be here. You're going to get me fired. I want that key you have. You can't be coming here anymore."

"What key. Christ, Garrett, anybody could walk in that back door . . ."

"Well, not anymore. I'm changing the lock. You're not coming . . ."

Baby John didn't like the rough toweling from the paper towels and began whimpering, then broke into a real rebuke to the whole process and announced it in lung howling wails.

"What the hell . . ." Garrett froze while Roger moved to

put himself between Garrett and Boone's shower stall.

"It's all right, we'll be out of here in just a minute."

"You brought a woman and a baby in here?" Garrett yelled. Boone finished with the diapering process, talking softly to the baby, then wrapping him back in his blankets and grabbed the non-nutritional sucking pacifier and jammed it in Baby John's mouth.

"It's not a woman, Garrett. Jesus, you think I'd bring a woman in here?"

Boone, fully dressed now himself, opened the shower stall and stood in the doorway holding the baby in his arms. He saw the man Garrett then, a tall, black man who looked like some actor Boone had seen in the movies. He was dressed in a gray combination of pants and shirt and a military-like cap. He looked more scared than angry.

"Name's Boone," Boone said. "This is my baby. His mother didn't want him."

"What the hell . . ." Garrett said again.

He turned then to face Roger. "You got to go," he said. "Whoever the hell they are, you've got to go."

Boone walked closer to him and Garrett looked at Baby John as if he was a rattlesnake or something dangerous.

"Garrett, you know what this building was supposed to be," Roger said.

"But ain't. We've been over that, Roger, dammit. I'm hired by the construction company to see that nobody comes in here that ain't supposed to be in here."

Roger looked at Boone. "The government built this place for veterans like me. Was supposed to put in rooms and kitchen and all that stuff for guys coming back from Iraq that had no place to go. A place for veterans like me. Like a lot of us."

Boone didn't understand. He looked at Garrett. "Wasn't any money appropriated for it," Garrett said. "Construction company rented it and that's who's using the place now."

"Construction company owned by the Senator's brother-in-law," Roger said.

Garrett stole another glance at the baby. "Po-lice looking for you?" he asked Boone.

Boone thought about an answer. "Not that I know about."

"Well, you can't be here," Garrett said. He took his military-like cap off and slammed it against his leg. "Dammit, Roger. I'm going to have to change the lock on that door. They find out you can just walk in off the street and use their facilities, I get fired."

"I don't want you to get fired, Garrett," Roger said.

"I know, I know," Garrett said.

Boone had Baby John tucked into the red basket again. Roger moved toward the door and Boone followed. As he walked past Garrett, Roger held the key he had used in the back door in his hand and offered it to Garrett. Garrett put his cap back on his head, looked at the key, but didn't take it.

"We're having breakfast at McDonald's," Roger said. "Want me to bring you an Egg McMuffin?"

"Not this time," Garrett said. He walked out the door ahead of Roger. Walking away from them he said, "Maybe next time."

5

TWO DOORS down from the restroom, Roger stopped. He watched as the man Garrett left the restroom, looked at them, at Roger smiling and waving a hand, then shook his head and went on down the hallway and out of sight.

Roger opened the door he stood by, looked in, then waved for Boone to follow him. Inside the room stood two brilliant white washing machines—GE label on them—and two clothes dryers with the same label. Roger began taking off his clothes—the olive fatigues and dingy gray Kansas City Chiefs boxer shorts and undershirt. He tossed all his clothes into one of the washers and turned, completely naked, to Boone. He pointed at Boone's jeans.

"You want to wash them Levis and your other stuff, peel 'em off and toss them in. Baby clothes, too."

He turned back to the washer, turned some knobs and it began filling with water. Over the washer shelves held various jugs and boxes. Roger selected one box, pushed up the flap and poured a handful of soap powder into the machine. He turned back around, noticed Boone had not moved, and said, "Hurry up you want to wear clean clothes into Big Mac's place don't you?"

Boone wasn't sure what to do. He had taken off his

clothes in front of others plenty of times in the boys' locker room at school, but Roger was a stranger and a man. That was different from school. He began stripping out of his clothes, hesitated when he got to his underwear, then, kind of turning away from Roger, stepped out of his Jockey shorts which were getting a bit stiff, and walked over to the washer and tossed everything in. Roger was taking the blankets out of the baby's basket, then slipped the smock off the baby with careful hands, surprising Boone how softly he handled Baby John.

Roger tossed the baby's stuff in the washer as he held the baby in one arm. He turned back to Boone and said, "How about the things in your bag, there?"

Boone was still cautious about Roger handling Baby John, about holding him, but the baby seemed happy enough, looking at Roger with the same blue eyed-stare he used on Boone. Shuffling through the articles in the bag, Boone decided everything needed a good washing so he dumped it all in with everything else and the three of them stood, watching the washer, completely naked except for Baby John's Pampers. Roger felt of the diaper and said, "Wet," then peeled it off and threw it in a nearby trash can.

The three naked males stood looking at each other and Roger began to laugh. "Look at us," he said, "three naked jay birds. Old Garrett catches us like this he'll shit his pants."

Boone began to see humor in the whole scene and joined in Roger's laughter. Roger began to dance around, swinging Baby John with the metal stump tapping against the concrete floor. Baby John's eyes went from Roger to Boone and soon a smile broke out on his chubby face and Roger howled. "Look at that. Look at that. Little Baby John, he's laughing too."

This was the first time Boone had seen a smile on the baby's face. He couldn't stop laughing, but he couldn't stop the tears from forming either, or stop them from running down his cheeks. The three of them continued their dance until they grew tired and the laughter stopped and all three of them sat down on the concrete floor on their bare butts, little Baby John between Roger and Boone, Boone's arm around his back until he realized the baby was sitting without support.

"Look, Roger," Boone said. "Look at that. Baby John can sit by himself."

Roger looked at the baby and smiled. "You're growing up, son. Let me give you one piece of advice. Don't ever join the Army."

6

THE GREASY aroma of McDonalds' fries stirred a hunger in Boone. He selected a table by the window, away from other customers, and set the basket and Baby John in one of the empty chairs. An older woman and man sat nearby, both watching Boone and the baby. Boone walked to the divider and trash receptacle and took the copy of the day's *Tribune*, smiling at the couple as he walked by.

Roger came to the table with a tray of food. The couple turned their attention to him and focused on his metal leg. He placed a wrapped Egg McMuffin in front of Boone, then an oil-oozing hashbrown clump half-wrapped in an oval shape followed by a small container of orange juice.

"And here's an orange juice for John," Roger said, handing another container to Boone.

"I don't have any way of giving it to him," Boone said.

"He's big enough to start drinking," Roger said and came around the table, took the orange juice from Boone, tore off the top, kneeled down with the metal leg extended behind him, held Baby John's head and tipped the bottle enough for a taste of the juice to run onto the baby's lips.

"Look at that, he likes it," Roger said.

Boone looked on skeptically.

"Be careful, Roger . . ." he began, but Roger tipped the bottle again, and again the baby licked his lips then smacked them hungrily. Roger tipped the bottle farther and juice ran into the baby's mouth and down the front of his gown.

"Be careful . . ." Boone repeated, Roger tipped the bottle farther still and the baby tasted, drank and began coughing. Followed by crying.

"Too much, he's choking," Boone said, alarmed, and began lifting the baby from the basket as his wailing became louder.

The woman who had been sitting nearby and watching intently, now was beside Boone and lifting the baby from his arms.

"My goodness," she said as she patted Baby John on the back, "you boys got this baby all choked up."

Baby John coughed, then leaned back, tears streaming from his eyes and stared at the woman. Boone was frozen, unable to move.

"This your baby brother?" the woman asked Boone. He nodded.

Roger stepped forward, "It's all right, ma'am. I'm the baby's daddy."

Baby John continued his intermittent coughing with more wailing. The woman's back-patting increased. She gave Roger a scolding look.

"Seems to me you ain't been taking care of this baby much."

A teenaged clerk in a McDonald smock and army type red and blue cap atop her mesh enclosed blonde hair appeared at the table and asked if she could do something to help.

"Well," the woman said, "he needs a drink of water." She looked at Boone. "You got him any clean water?"

"Uh," Boone responded, still a bit in shock, "I don't have any clean bottles for him."

A man in shirt and tie with a Big Mac arch on the tie was there at the table. "Linda," looking at the blonde teenager, "I think we have a clean baby bottle on one of the shelves that someone left here. Find it and see that it's sterilized."

Roger said, "We best be going," but the man said, "No, no, it's all right, we'll take care of our young customers."

Several other people were gathering around the table now. A portly woman in faded dress and unevenly cut hair said, "Where'd you get that baby, Roger?"

Roger said, "Shut up, Sadie."

A girl, middle teens, with an outdated punk style haircut and a purple pompadour walked up to Boone and smiled at him. Boone glanced at her for a moment before focusing back on Baby John who was whimpering now. He did notice the gold studs in the girl's nostrils, the string of rings hanging from one ear plus the one in one eyebrow just below a tattoo.

The blonde McDonalds' employee returned in a hurry holding a plastic baggie with a baby bottle inside and a bottle of water in the other hand. She gave it to the man in the McDonald tie who held it out to the woman holding the baby. The woman, looking sternly at Boone now, said, "Well, take the bottle. Pour the damn water in it. Get this baby something to drink."

Boone fumbled with the bottle, suddenly nervous, barely able to keep from dropping the whole combination. Roger took the bottle and the water from him and proceeded to get it ready for the baby. The woman grabbed the bottle from him with her free hand and thrust the nipple into Baby John's mouth stifling his screams. He sucked on the bottle greedily.

"Well," the man with the tie said, "crisis over. Have a good day and thanks for coming to McDonald's." With a wave of the hand he departed. The blonde girl looked confused, smiled at Boone and scampered after the man with the tie.

The woman Roger had called Sadie said, "Roger where'd you get the damn baby?"

Roger ignored her. The girl with the purple hair was now beside Boone and faking an accidental move, rubbed him with both her protruding breasts which threatened to bust out of a tie-dyed orange tank top.

Roger sat at the table and said, "Let's get them McMuffins wolfed down before they get cold."

The woman holding the baby looked at Boone. "You think you can handle him now?"

"Yes, ma'am, I can," Boone said and lifted the baby from her arms. Baby John came up for air and smiled at Boone around the nipple still in his mouth.

The woman stood there for another minute watching Boone, watching to see he held the baby properly, watching to see that the baby didn't start squalling again. She turned and went back to the booth where the man sat drinking a free refill of senior coffee.

The woman Sadie sat in the chair next to Roger and the

48

punk-haired girl lifted the red Target basket with the baby stuff inside and set it on the floor, then seated herself. Boone remained standing, holding Baby John who decided to drink some more water. The girl said to Boone, "What's your name?"

Before he could respond, Sadie asked him, "You want I could hold the baby so's you could eat your breakfast."

Boone didn't respond.

The girl stood and looked directly into Boone's face. "What's your name?"

"Leave him alone, Berkely, can't you see he's busy," from Roger.

"Where the hell'd the baby come from?" Sadie demanded.

Berkely leaned in closer. "What's the baby's name?"

Roger wrapped up his half-eaten McMuffin, stuffed it in the sack along with his hashbrowns, reached across the table and did the same with Boone's. He stacked up the drinks, took the sack and said to Boone, "Come on, let's go where it's quieter."

"Where you stayin'," Sadie asked. "You still sleeping in the park or down under the bridge? We got us a nice place in the Salvation Army building. They got more room, come on over there. Don't cost anything."

"I don't like the company," Roger said, walking away. Boone stepped around Berkely and gathered up Baby John's belongings, placed them in the red basket with his free hand, clutching the baby tightly against him with the other hand. Berkely didn't move aside to make it easier for him.

"Who's the baby's momma?" she asked. "Where's the

baby's momma live? Are you really the baby's brother?"

"The Tee Vee says there's a baby missing in Eldon," Sadie said and Boone's heart banged against his ribs. He moved quickly to follow Roger out the door. Behind him Sadie shouted, "That ain't him is it?"

THEY WERE back in the building where they'd showered. Roger went to one of the picnic style tables in the break room, took the food out of the bag and took it to the microwave and turned it on.

"Don't have nothing to do with Sadie or Berkely," he told Boone. "They try to get you to have sex. It's all they think about."

Boone sat and put Baby John down in his blankets inside the basket, sound asleep.

"I'm going to have to get some more formula and some diapers for the baby," he told Roger.

Roger took the food out of the microwave and returned to the table. "You got any money?"

Boone started on the McMuffin to stave off his hunger. "Not much."

"I've got a bank account. My disability check goes in it. I got, oh, maybe a thousand dollars there. I've got this debit card thing we can buy stuff with."

"I don't have any way to pay you back," Boone told him.

"I don't loan money," Roger said. Boone stared quizzically. "Long as you're with me, it's your money, too. Your's and Baby John's."

Boone didn't speak for a moment, knowing his voice

would break up if he did. Then he said, "I'm going to make you Baby John's godfather, Roger."

Roger looked at the sleeping baby. "I got a pocket full of medals someplace. Being Baby John's godfather beats all of them. I'm honored, Boone. Thank you."

Boone smiled as he nodded and chewed the last of his breakfast. Life had calmed for him, he had a friend, he felt confident about caring for the baby and no one as far as he knew was looking for him. One slight dread lingered inside him, the fact that the missing baby from Eldon had become known to just about everyone.

7

FRANK GRIFFIN stopped his Lincoln pickup next to the cement truck with a long loading chute trailing from the rear. A steady stream of viscous cement raced down the chute into a geometric form where a half-dozen men stood waiting to smooth the concrete after the pouring. Griffin looked across the space at Jack Blakely, one of the concrete finishers standing there, and motioned to him. He then turned and walked to the Lincoln. When Blakely came up to him, Griffin motioned toward his truck and said, "Get in."

When they had both settled into leather seats in front and closed the doors, Griffin asked, "Where's the boy?"

"You mean my son?" Jack Blakely asked.

"Yes."

"I don't know."

Griffin turned to look at Blakely then. He was a large man of stern visage and with a generally disapproving air about him. He sniffed loudly as if wanting Blakely to notice. "You been drinking already this morning, Jack?"

Blakely stared back at him, saying nothing.

"Your son took the baby, didn't he?" Griffin asked.

"My son left home," Blakely said. "Seems everyone at his school enjoyed calling him Daddy."

"Well, he committed a crime. The baby is only six months old. The couple from Iowa came here to adopt him, give him a decent home. Someplace people won't be talking about him every day. I suspect you know where he took the baby and who's got him now. What's he doing, holding him for you and your wife?"

"Boone left us a note, said he had to leave because he couldn't live here any longer in this town. He's a man now, he can take care of himself."

"No, he's a boy. He's a boy who committed a terrible sin. He can't run away from that. He can't run away from God."

Blakely said, "Where's your daughter, Frank? Where's the baby's mother?"

"You know where she is. She's at a Baptist school back East. She's got herself right with God. She pays for her sin every day and God has accepted her back into his graces. But she can't come back here. Not as long as that boy of yours is all people are talking about. And the baby. I don't want that boy coming back here and bringing that baby and stirring everybody up again."

"I don't think Boone will be coming back here. I told him to be a man about this, he's not a boy any longer."

"So you told him to leave?"

"No. Not directly. But he's brought a lot of scorn and ridicule into our life."

Blakely was silent for a moment, then, "My wife has started drinking again. Pretty bad. I don't know what to do about it."

"And you're drinking, too?"

Blakely nodded. "Some, yes. Not like before."

"I gave you this job, Jack. Two years ago. You promised you would stop the liquor. That you would go to church. Get back with God. You haven't been to church for almost six months. Since the baby was born."

"I'm still trying," Blakely said. He looked through the windshield of the truck, into the distance. "Everything was going along all right until . . . well, until all this mess came up."

Griffin too stared into the distance, both of them sitting quiet and unmoving. Griffin said, "I can't let you stay here in this town, Jack. I can't have that boy of yours walking the street reminding everyone of what he did, of that baby. He means to bring the baby back, thinking you and your wife can raise the baby. I can't have that. I have a job in progress in El Dorado Springs. You and your wife can move there, you want. You're living in the house I rent to you so it shouldn't be a problem for you to move."

Blakely looked at him, but Griffin continued to stare through the windshield of the truck.

"What?" Blakely asked. "What are you saying? You're what, firing me from this job?"

"If you don't want the job there you'll have to move out of my house. Your chances of finding another job in this town are not too good. You'll adjust down there. When the boy comes back to you and brings the baby, I'll try to keep him out of jail. But he has to give the baby back. Back to be adopted and out of the state. I don't want any more publicity about the baby, I want to keep it quiet. I know the sheriff and I have him looking for that boy and the baby. If he makes this a nationwide alert—one of those Amber Alerts—some-body's going to jail. Think about it. I don't want any of you ever to come back to Eldon again."

8

THREE DAYS had passed since the incident with Sadie
and Berkely in McDonalds. The nights under the bridge were
quiet, but cool. Roger went for food—sometimes back to
McDonalds, sometimes to the grocery. They showered and
ate in the building Roger said was supposed to be for veterans. Once Garrett came into the room where they were eating and told Roger he was going to have to change the locks
on the doors, but he never did. He even smiled at Baby John
who smiled back.

The baby grew every day. Boone began to get the hang
of caring for a baby, recognizing his every sign for food, for
sleep, for a warm bath. When the baby slept and when Roger
was out for food or diapers or other baby supplies, Boone
spent time trying to figure out what to do, how to plan his
future and the future for Baby John. Going home was not an
option. He had come to accept his parents as they were. He
knew they had gone through some bad times with their
drinking and he remembered too well the late night shouting
when he had to bury his head in the pillows to stifle the
sound. But they had never been abusive to him.

Here he was, sixteen. Old enough to get a driver's li-

cense. All the other boys in Eldon who were sixteen would
be out driving their father's car or truck except the really rich
among them and they would be looking at cars on the lots
for their parents to buy for them. If he had a car he and Baby
John could just take off and see the world. Maybe take Roger
with them. Yes, definitely take Roger.

Why had Penny come back to Eldon to have the baby?
Even before her stomach gave away her condition, her parents had sent her back East to some religious school. At
night after his lights were out and after the Wii was turned
off, after—he was sure—everyone else in the whole town
was asleep, he would wonder what kind of baby Penny
would have and if he would ever get to see it. The notion that
he was the father of a living human being was at first alarm-
ing to him. Then, when he found out the baby was a boy, he
began to imagine himself as a father. Someone who would
train the boy in all the things he liked to do. Someone to
walk beside with his arm around and for perhaps the very
first time in his life Boone understood the meaning of love.

But it had been in the Catholic hospital in Jefferson City
where Baby John came into the world. Penny left town,
never trying to talk with Boone, never contacting even the
gang of kids her age she had associated with. But, the town
knew. Small towns do not keep secrets, no matter how hard
the Griffins tried to keep it secret. No one approached them
about Penny and the baby as far as Boone knew. But everyone knew. And they took it out on him.

On the day Roger was late returning from the store
Boone took Baby John down to the river to look at the turtles
and the occasional fish jumping out of the water. He watched

several boats going by and remembered what Roger had said about taking one of the boats down the river to New Orleans. He pictured himself and Baby John in New Orleans. Entering Baby John in school. Watching him grow up. Teaching him how to skateboard. How to draw and sketch. Then the thought of a mother for Baby John entered his mind. Since his encounter with Penny in the front seat of her car, he had not dated another girl. He was uncomfortable in their presence. He shied away from any knowledge about girls, especially sexual knowledge. Once he Googled the birth of a baby and was amazed how a girl like Penny could adapt their body to carry a baby inside and even more amazed at how a woman's orifice could expand to the size of a baby's head.

The sun disappeared into the river and the colors in the sky splashed across the waves in the water. If only he had his pastels, what a sketch he could make. Baby John slept through the show of nature with Boone wanting to show him what beauty existed in his world. He wanted badly to share this moment with someone and for the first time since meeting Roger, loneliness set in.

He walked back to their almost-home under the bridge expecting Roger to be there, but, no Roger. Boone fixed a bottle for the baby then fed him the last jar of applesauce he had. One bun and one slice of bologna was all that was left in his pack. If Roger didn't hurry up and get back he would have to return in the dark and with his metal leg that could be a little dangerous for him.

As darkness came on and no Roger he fixed his sleeping bag and laid Baby John down, but the baby wasn't ready to sleep. He waved his hands and drooled a bit and tried his best to talk. Boone talked with him for a while, telling him about the sunset and the red sky that turned orange and yellow and finally many shades of gray. The baby watched him closely, responding to the sound of Boone's voice with his hands and his eyes. Then he closed his eyes and fell asleep. Darkness came in a rush and Boone was unsure what to do. Where could Roger be? The traffic noise on the bridge above them was still and the night became silent. No night birds. No boats on the river. The silence became fearful and Boone pulled the baby closer to him afraid there might be something or someone out there in the night, in the quiet, that would harm them. Once he thought he heard a sound like someone walking and he almost called out to Roger, but the sound never repeated. The time was very late, the night very dark and very still. Boone's heart beat rapidly and putting his hand on Baby John's chest and felt his tiny heart beating. Now in harmony, Boone drifted off to sleep.

The baby woke him before daylight. He held him close and rocked back and forth with him, but the baby continued to whimper. Boone had nothing more to give him, not even water. When the crying started he felt sure it would arouse someone and they would either hurt them both or call the police.

Maybe he would have to go home when it became daylight. If he did he knew they would take Baby John away from him and he would never see his son again. The thoughts of his problems, of the baby's problems, would have terrified him and sent him to tears, as it had when he had walked into the church ready to give up on his dreams. But his father told him he had to be a man, no more crying.

He bent and kissed his son on his forehead and the baby's crying stopped. He sang silly songs he remembered from his own, now distant childhood. As his hopes rose, so did the rising sun at the other end of the river. Baby John slept again. Boone searched his pockets and came up with a dollar and forty-five cents. Not enough for food for the baby. Dammit Roger, where are you? He gathered up all of his belongings and the baby's and picked up the red Target basket which the baby was now beginning to outgrow, and he started for the metal building where they had been eating and taking showers. He had nowhere else to go.

But wait. What about Roger's stuff? Should he leave it? He went back to the place where Roger stuffed his meager belongings behind some bushes next to the concrete bridge support. The satchel Roger always carried with him when he went shopping was there behind the rolled up sleeping bag and the duffel bag of clothes. Boone opened the satchel, looked inside and there were the keys to the back door of the metal building. And Roger's trifold billfold he always carried with him. Inside the billfold Boone saw the debit card without which Roger would have been unable to purchase anything. Why had he gone off without it? Where did he go? What had he said when he left. Boone remembered Roger mumbling something, but he hadn't understood and hadn't asked him to repeat it. He had assumed Roger was going to the store so he had called out to him to remember food for Baby John.

Boone worried then about what could have happened.

He knew what he had to do. Find Roger.

9

THE KEY slid into the lock and Boone hoped that Garrett had not changed the lock as he had repeatedly threatened Roger he would do. He felt the lock when it clicked, slowly he opened the door. The baby slept in his basket as Boone picked him up and went inside. In the room where he and Roger had often spread their food on one of the tables to eat, he placed the groceries he had purchased at the convenience store with Roger's debit card. The man in the store had seen him there often and assumed he was Roger's son, had asked if Boone knew his dad's password and laughed when Boone said he forgot it.

"Good thing I remembered, then," the man said. He chatted away as he rang up the items Boone purchased, asking how his father was and was he at work. Boone answered in single syllables.

Before he and the baby finished their meal, Garrett came into the room. Boone didn't know what to expect. Garrett, clearly displeased to see him there, looked all around the room, then backed into the hallway to look both ways. He came back inside and closed the door.

"Where's Roger?" he asked.

Boone, reluctant to admit he didn't know for fear Garrett would make him leave, shrugged.

Garrett looked at the food on the table, at Baby John now sucking on his bottle of apple juice.

"Is he here?" Garrett asked.

Boone shook his head.

"Where the hell is he?"

Boone shrugged again.

"Look, you two going to have to stop this. I'm fixing to get my ass fired you keep coming in here."

Maybe it was the look on Boone's face or maybe it was the tears he felt in his eyes and the moisture he had to look through that changed Garrett, made him come forward and stand close enough to Boone to touch him, made him soften his voice. "He sick?"

Boone could do no more than shake his head.

"Damn, he's having another one of them attacks of his ain't he?"

Barely above a whisper, Boone said, "I don't know." He rubbed his hand across his nose that was running now, down on his top lip, into his mouth. "He's gone, Garrett. He left all his stuff. I don't know what to do."

Garrett watching him, backed away, shook his head. "Aw, hell. He's out of it again. I better call and see if he's made it to the hospital."

He took out his cell phone and began dialing. He talked with two hospitals, telling them he was looking for his friend a veteran named Roger and had he checked into the emergency room. He was told no, both places.

He sat at the table across from Boone. "You know what's

wrong with him, don't you?"

"Well, he has a metal leg," Boone said.

"He's got more metal in his head." Garrett walked away shaking his head again. At the door he stopped. "I'll call the VA office here. If he didn't show up there like he does sometimes . . .he ain't there . . . he ain't been to the VA he's probably lying in the street somewhere."

"What can we do?" Boone asked. He stood, a rising in his chest troubled him. He saw Garrett's anxiety, started feeling it himself.

Garrett came back and sat down, motioning Boone to be seated. He began dialing the phone again. He asked the same question, waited and asked, "When?" Waited again, then, "How bad is he?"

A lump came in Boone's throat. He was no longer hungry. He put the rest of his sandwich back in the bag while Garrett was putting his phone away in his pocket.

"He been there," Garrett said. "Had to take him to Columbia to the Harry Truman VA Hospital there."

"What . . . what happened to him?"

Garrett shrugged. "He gets these attacks sometimes. I let him sleep them off in here when it's bad outside. He stays in the hospital for a few days and they turn him back out on the street. Man's got some serious problems."

"What can we do?"

"Ain't nothing *we* can do. VA needs to treat him, but he don't want to stay in no damn hospital. Can't blame him."

"Will they keep him?"

"He won't stay. He's a stubborn mother . . . he's stubborn."

Baby John was finished with his bottle now and Boone picked him up and balanced him on one shoulder, waiting for the burp to come.

"Could I . . .I would like to see him in the hospital."

"It's in Columbia, kid, don't you understand? Fifty miles away."

"I'm Boone, Garrett. This is Baby John. Roger's our friend. I think he's your friend, too. We need to see him."

10

HE HAD to ask only once the location of the Salvation Army home. Inside the front door on the first floor he inquired from a woman in a fairly clean dress where Sadie and Berkely's room was. Third floor, the woman said. The house was old, the stairs worn from many shoe soles. On the third floor he was confronted with three doors, picked one and knocked on it. The door opened and Berkely stood there. She looked at him, grinned real big, then looked at the basket and the baby.

"Oh, look, you brought the baby for us to see," she said and reached down to pick Baby John up from the basket. At first, the baby didn't like it, but didn't cry out.

"Look, Ma," Berkely called out. "It's that boy that was with Roger with the baby."

Sadie came waddling to the door. She saw the baby who was scrunching his face ready to cry out, looked at Boone, then reached to take the baby from Berkely.

Baby John whimpered once, puzzzled about what was going on. Sadie held him to her ample bosom and stroked his head.

"Hey, little feller," she said, "them men been treating you all right? You need a mama's care?"

Berkely took Boone by the arm and pulled him inside

the room. A few pieces of worn furniture filled up the small room. Boone saw a small kitchen area to one side and an open door showed an unmade bed.

Sadie said, "You really this baby's brother?"

Boone just nodded. Berkely said, "We're fixing to go down to McDonald's for some lunch. Want to come?"

Boone swallowed hard, still unsure of what he was doing. "Roger's in the hospital in Columbia. I was going to go see him. They won't let babies in so I was wondering if you could keep him until I get back. Should be by four or five o'clock."

Berkely clasped her hands together and turned to Sadie. "Oh, Mama, can we keep him? Huh, can we Mama?"

Sadie held the baby out and looked at him. "What is he five, six months old?"

"More like eight," Boone said. "He still sleeps most of the day. He won't be any bother. I've brought food and drinks for him. And clean bottles. Diapers, everything you'll need."

"Where's his mama?" Sadie asked.

"She ran off," Boone said. "Just me and Roger to raise him. Soon as Roger gets out of the hospital I'll be getting a job."

"You sure he ain't no kidnapped baby?" Sadie asked.

"No, he belongs to me now. I mean both of us. I'll be the main one to raise him, I guess."

"Uhh," Sadie said. "All right, then. We'll keep him. Long as we don't get into any trouble over it."

"No M'am, you won't get into any trouble."

Berkely was jumping up and down and clapping her

hands. "Oh goodie. That's just grand. A baby. Let me hold him, Mama."

"Sit down over there so's you don't drop him, " Sadie said.

Boone watched them a while, trying to make sure in his mind he wasn't making a mistake leaving his baby with the two women. Less than sure, almost changed his mind, but knew that if he did he might never see Roger again. He owed it to him to go to the hospital. Garrett had promised to drive him to Columbia and bring him back in time for Garrett's shift at work.

"Please take good care of him," he said as he backed out the door. "He means a lot to me. And to Roger."

"Don't you worry none," Sadie said, looking at him. "I'll treat him like he was one of my own."

THE HARRY TRUMAN VA hospital was a maze of offices, cubicles and doorways. Garrett knew where to go so Boone followed him through the corridors. On the way to Columbia Garrett had tried to engage him in conversation, asking about the baby, about him, about his relationship with Roger. Boone answered in short syllables, hating to telling outright lies, but feeling that telling the truth about Baby John would lose him.

They found Roger in a room with four other men. Two of them asleep, two others, wan of face with black and gray stubble covering the lower half, had their eyes on Roger who was sitting in his bed, covered with a gray blanket with a strap over the top restraining him to the bed. Roger's reddish brown hair now uncombed and stuck up and out in all directions. His voice was loud and agitated, expounding on his situation at the hospital.

He looked at Boone and Garrett as they entered the door and his mouth stopped moving, his wild eyes calmed, then expressed joy.

"Is that you? Is that you?" he kept repeating. Boone walked ahead of Garrett and stood by Roger's bed, a smile on his face, a bit of fear rising in his throat.

"Hello Roger," he said. "How are you?"

"My God, my God, it's you. It's the boy. It's . . . yes, by God, it's Boone. It is, isn't it? Boone?"

"It's me," Boone said, his smile bigger.

Garrett, at the bed now, said, "Roger, how you doin' Man?"

"My God, my God," Roger turned to the two patients who were still watching him, their faces remaining emotionless. "Look boys. These are my two best friends. Boone and . . .Boone and Garrett. It's Garrett, right?"

Garrett nodded. "Boy wanted to come see you. Drove him up. Have to get back in a couple of hours. Have to guard that big building from people just walkin' in."

"My God, my God. You two, driving all the way up here just to see me. I'll be damned. I thought I was stuck here forever and you two came to get me out of this jail they got me in."

"Yeah, well, we'll see about getting you out in a few days," Garrett said. "We'll talk with your doctor about that."

"Don't pay any attention to the damn doctor, they don't know anything." He reached out to touch Boone's arm. "The baby? What was his name, Baby John? You bring him with you?"

Boone said, "No, I left him with a baby sitter. Are you doing okay, Roger?"

"Sure, sure. Fit as a fiddle. Have to come in this joint every so often, have them check my blood pressure, that sort of thing, you know."

At Roger's urging, Boone brought him up to date on Baby John, and when Boone told him who he had left the baby with, Roger shouted, "No, no, you didn't. Not that damn Sadie and her crazy daughter Berkely. You can't trust them."

Boone took it like a jab in the gut. "Why?"

"All that damn Berkely talks about is having a baby? She ask you to have sex with her and give *her* a baby?"

"No."

"Well, look, you better get back and get your baby back. Don't ever leave your baby with those two crazy women."

"Well, I . . ." Boone looked at Garrett.

"I'll get you back, don't worry, kid," Garrett said. "When you think they'll let you go, Roger?"

"I'm through," Roger said. "You want to get my leg for me? I think they put it in that locker over there against the wall." He pointed to a metal locker painted white along the wall opposite Roger's bed.

Garrett said, "Maybe we better wait . . ."

"No, it's all right. Just get the leg for me."

Garrett said, pointing at the strap over Roger's bed. "How you going to get out from under that?"

"See if you can unbuckle it," Roger said, tugging at the

wide, heavy strap. One of the men who had been watching Roger started laughing.

"You ain't going anywhere," he said in a coarse voice. "You're crazy like the rest of us. You ain't never gettin' out of old Hairy Ass Truman alive."

Roger jerked his head around and said to the man, "Hell I'm not. The rest of you are the crazy ones. Ain't nothing wrong with me. Just a headache." He looked at Garrett and Boone. "Never should have gone into the clinic at Jeff. Thought they would just give me the pills. Said I had to come here for the prescription. Lied to me. Said I had the Post Traumatic Syndrome. That's what they say about all of us been over there. No cure for it, though."

"You feeling okay now, Roger?" Boone asked.

"Yeah, hell yes. Gave me the pills, headache's gone, I feel good as new. Except I need the leg."

"We'll check with the doctor, Roger," Garrett said.

"Shoot him, shoot him," the patient who had been laughing at him shouted. "He's crazier'n hell. Shoot him."

"Shut up," Roger shouted back at him.

A nurse in white appeared at the door. "What's going on in here?" she asked.

"Shoot him, shoot him," the man kept shouting.

"Shut him up," Roger said, pointing at the man.

The nurse walked to the bed where the man was struggling to get out from under the strap across his bed. She said something to him as she gently, but firmly pushed him back down onto his bed. She pulled the blanket over him and stroked his head a few times. She came to Roger's bed and looking at Garrett and Boone, said, "Visiting time is over."

"Over? Over?" Roger said. "They just got here."

Looking at Garrett she said, "You'll need to go."

Garrett nodded. To Roger he said, "Get well, Man. I'll help you find a place back in Jeff so's you won't have to sneak into my building anymore."

Boone said, "We miss you, Roger. Me and Baby John."

Roger looked a bit bewildered. Boone said, "I used your debit card for some baby food. I'll try and pay you back."

"It's okay," Roger said. To the nurse he said, "Maybe if they stay just another five minutes . . . "

"Visiting hours are up, Roger. They can come back to-morrow."

Garrett walked toward the door and Boone followed. At the door Boone turned back and said, "Bye Roger. We'll come back again. Get well."

Roger looked strickened as if he'd suffered a blow to the head. He was still staring after them as they walked out the door.

Going down the hall to the elevator Garrett said, "I don't know. It's goin' to be awhile before they let Roger out of here."

As they reached the elevator, Garrett punched the down button and while they waited, he looked at Boone and said, "I know cause I spent two months in here myself."

GARRETT SAID they should go to the cafeteria for a lunch before going back.

"Food ain't bad," he told Boone. "Better than McDonalds."

As they ate sandwiches and chips, Boone worried about Baby John. He didn't think Sadie or Berkely would hurt Baby John. Both of them seemed to like the baby and he was confident they knew how to take care of him and feed him with the food he had left them.

Garrett led the way back to the revolving front door, speaking to several hospital employees on the way. He told Boone he remembered some of the people there.

"Treated me all right," he said.

Garrett's faded red pickup was in the front row in the parking lot so they found it easily. Inside, Garrett started the truck and backed it out of the parking space and drove out of the lot, back onto Highway 63 toward Jefferson City when a voice from the back seat of the truck said "Just keep driving."

Garrett looked into the rearview mirror. "Roger, what the hell you doin' in my truck?"

11

ROGER TALKED incessantly on the way to Jefferson City. Boone expected Garrett to turn around and take Roger back to the hospital, but he didn't. Roger made it sound as if he had been tortured in the psychiatric ward. He laughingly told them how he had slithered out from under the strap on his bed, retrieved his metal leg, sneaked past the nurses' station by sliding the metal foot instead of clanking it on the floor. He was so amused at his own stories Garrett and Boone could not help but laugh along with him

They stopped under the bridge after crossing the river where Roger retrieved his clothes from his stash beside a bridge support. He stripped out of the hospital gown—Boone wondering how he sneaked past the security guards at the revolving door in a gown—and came back to the truck. Garrett told Boone he would take him by the Salvation Army house where he had left Baby John, then Garrett needed to get to work.

At the house Boone said to Garrett, "Be right back," as he jumped out of the truck. He took the stairs to the apartment two at a time where he had left Baby John with Sadie and Berkely and prepared to knock on the door.

The door stood ajar.

Panic followed. Boone pushed the door open, called to Sadie, then Berkely, and got no response. Something different in the room, not like he had left it. Looking around, seeing nothing that would belong to either Sadie or Berkely. He went into the bedroom where the bed was disheveled, but no bedclothes, no shoes, no luggage. He went to the small closet where the door stood open. Completely empty.

He walked through the whole apartment again, now with his skin burning, a large lump in his throat, an empty feeling in his stomach. He left the apartment, ran down the stairs and stopped in front of the door with the number one on it. He knocked on the door repeatedly until an older woman opened it looking frightened.

Breathless he said, "Sadie, Sadie," his voice catching in his throat. "Where is Sadie? Where is Berkely?"

The woman clutched at her throat. "Why . . . why they've gone to the train station."

"The train station? Today?"

"About an hour ago. Is . . .is something wrong?"

"They had a baby with them?"

"Why yes. Sadie said they were taking the baby to St. Louis to his mother."

Boone leaned against the wall to hold himself up. His face was on fire and his eyes were becoming unfocused.

"Is something wrong?" the woman asked.

He left the building, his mind scrambled. Where was he? Where was he supposed to go? He heard Garrett calling him and he turned to see Garrett leaning out of the faded red truck window.

"Over here," Garrett said.

Boone stumbled his way over to the truck, stopping in front of Garrett, staring at him.

Garrett said, "What's wrong? What happened?"

Boone could barely get the words out. "They stole my baby. They kidnapped Baby John and they're taking him to St. Louis."

GARRETT DROVE faster than the speed limit on the way to the train station. Roger said, "I knew it. Those two are bad news. They couldn't wait to get their hands on that baby."

He put his hand on Boone's shoulder. "Don't worry good buddy, we'll get the baby back. Even if we have to go all the way to St. Louis."

Boone couldn't think. The image of Sadie holding Baby John occupied his thoughts. He couldn't erase the picture from his mind.

At the train station Garrett pulled in close to the building with one wheel on the sidewalk. Roger was out of the truck even before it stopped rolling, yelling for Boone to follow him. A uniformed conductor was picking up the steps before one entrance to the train and it started moving slowly.

Roger yelled, "Wait," and the conductor looked in their direction. Boone ran past Roger and his clanking metal leg. The conductor started waving his hands at them and Boone thought he meant for them to stop, but Boone ran even faster and grabbed the handle by the door to the train and swung up. The conductor grabbed his arm and pulled him inside. Roger was coming faster than Boone thought he could. The conductor yelled at him to hurry up and just before the train pulled away from him, Roger grabbed the bar, the conductor grabbed Roger and Boone reached past the conductor to grab Roger's shirt and together they pulled him on board.

"You ain't supposed to do that," the conductor said. "You lose your other leg trying that."

"Thanks," Roger told him. "We've got to get to St. Louis."

"You got tickets?" the conductor asked.

"We can buy tickets on board, can't we?" Roger asked.

"Well, yeah. Find you a seat and I'll be by later to get your money." The conductor started to move away and Roger asked, "You see two women with a baby get on? One of them with purple hair."

"I saw them go that way," the conductor said, pointing toward the front of the train.

Boone began moving in that direction before the conductor finished talking. He heard Roger's clanking foot behind him and heard him say, "Easy. Easy, Boone. We grab the baby on the train and the police will get involved."

Boone stopped, looked back at Roger. "What can we do, then?"

"First we locate them. When they announce the first stop—I think it's a town called Herman—then just before the train starts up, we grab Baby John and hop off the train before they can stop us. I don't think they'll start anything on the train. After all, they stole the baby."

Boone thought about it. Roger was probably right. That was the best way to do it.

They walked through two cars until Boone saw the top

of a purple head of hair. He stopped, pointed and Roger said, "Aha, there they are. Okay, let's settle in right here. The snack bar is in the next car and you can bet Sadie will be going there. Sit here, stay low, don't let them see us until the first stop."

Boone sat, but he couldn't prevent looking between the seats for Baby John. The train was gaining speed now and the river passed along on the left side. Boone divided his time looking out at the river and looking between the seats. The car was only about half filled with no one sitting in front of him and Roger. Roger took a magazine out of the back of the seat and flipped through the pages. When Boone looked back at the space between the seats he saw Sadie stand up, holding the baby. Baby John's face was scrunched as if he was going to let out a howl. Boone's hand shot out and he grabbed Roger's leg. Roger leaned over, saw Sadie and placed a finger in front of his mouth. Boone's pulse quickened.

"Okay," Roger said, "we've got to cool it till the first stop which ought to be about thirty minutes. What d'ya want to talk about?"

Boone could only think about the baby. "I don't know anything."

"Tell me how you got the baby. Said it was your's and they were going to adopt him out. So, where's the mom now. How'd you grab him?"

Boone told him how it started with Penny, about the first time, the story he told his dad. The true story. He told how Penny wouldn't leave him alone after that. How she dragged him past the guy she really had a crush on, Duke Mansfield, just to make him jealous. He told Roger how Penny had picked him up in her car and how they had done it again, two more times, then she ignored him. Duke got the message and they started hanging around together again.

"Soon as she starting showing they sent her away," he said. "She told some of her friends. That's when they all started calling me Daddy."

"So then, what? She came home with the baby?"

"She came back to Jefferson City to have the baby. Then they gave the baby away. Some woman in a little town kept him. I think they paid her and I think she was some relation to Penny's dad. They went through the adoption process and finally some couple in Iowa got to adopt him. The woman brought him back to Eldon for the couple to pick up. I was waiting outside the Griffin's house. I wanted to see the couple who were going to adopt him. But they didn't come there. The woman left the baby in the car while she ran into the house for something and . . . well, I don't know, I just went over to the car and drove off. I didn't even think about it.

"That was pretty brave of you, Boone," Roger said and that pleased Boone. "So you drove the car down to Jeff? Where'd you leave it?"

"No, I left it in Eldon at Wal Mart's. I called my friend Dewey and he drove me to Jeff."

"How'd you plan to live?"

"I didn't have any plans. I almost left him at the Catholic church, but I went back for him."

"You did the right thing," Roger told him. Boone checked on the women and the baby, but didn't see any of them except the top of Berkely's purple-tinted head darting around.

He grew fidgety then, he needed to go to the bathroom. He heard a small whimper from Baby John and again Roger cautioned him with the finger across his lips. When they heard the conductor coming from the front of the car, Roger said in a loud whisper, "Go to the restroom and stay there for ten minutes."

Boone found the restroom, locked himself in, used it, flushed—pushing the button as the signage ordered him to do—waited. He didn't count the minutes, but it seemed like forever. A knock on the door, heartbeat up, then silence. He waited longer, maybe five more minutes that seemed like an hour. He eased the door open, saw no one, and headed back to his seat one car away. Through the doors, feeling the sway of the train, then he entered the car where he had been sitting. No Roger.

Anxiety hit, then terror. Looking toward where Sadie and Berkely were sitting he saw the top of Berklely's purple hair and across the aisle, his metal leg out into the aisle, sat Roger. Roger with his hand waving at Boone, motioning him to stay back. Boone slid into the seat where Roger had been sitting, keeping his eyes toward Roger and the two women. Baby John could not be seen, where was he? He heard Roger, his voice carrying throughout the car, "So the kid gave you guys the baby, huh? That's odd. I don't know where he went off to. I had to go into the hospital for a few days. So what are you going to do with the baby?"

Sadie's voice, but Boone couldn't hear what she was saying. Then Roger again, "Oh, you're taking him back to his parents, huh? That's good. He belongs with his parents."

Sadie's voice again.

Roger: "Hey, I don't know who the kid is or where he came from. Or how he ended up with the baby."

When Roger tried to encourage Sadie and Berkely to go to the snack car and leave the baby with him, they must have declined that offer as they didn't leave.

Boone began to develop a plan of his own. Grab Baby John and run out of the car. Would Sadie yell for help that her baby had been kidnapped or was she afraid of police involvement?

The loud speaker announced that they would be stopping in four minutes at Herman. Boone sneaked a look at Roger and saw him holding four fingers in the air.

The longest four minutes Boone could ever remember spending had nearly passed—the clock seemingly stopped—before he felt the train slowing, the loud speaker announcing everyone disembarking at Herman should advance to the baggage car, two cars back of where they were. Now Boone had to make his move. He stood and saw Roger standing in the aisle. Roger stepped in front of Berkely, leaned over and took Baby John out of Sadie's arms. Boone was right by Roger now, his heart pounding in his chest, he took the baby from Roger, saw Sadie standing, Berkely wide-eyed, still sitting, Roger blocking both of them, Boone racing down the car carrying his baby who made no sound.

He heard the voices behind him, a loud screech from Sadie. People in the seats watched him go running by. He was quickly through the doors and the interchange between cars. He ran with no one trying to stop him. He came to the steps in the baggage car that led outside. The conductor had placed the steps for people getting off the train on the platform and stood by them speaking to people as they stepped down. With no one in front of him on the steps and no one behind him, Boone stepped off the train and the conductor looked at him.

"Did you . . .is that your baby? Hold on there, young man . . ." but Boone was gone toward the station on a run. He heard voices and commotion behind him, but he dared not stop. He was out on the street now, in the dark, and saw a car with a TAXI sign in the front window. He opened the back door of the car, got in, and out of breath said to the driver, "Drive up by the station, my dad is coming."

When the taxi got to the front of the station, a mob of people spilled out of the doors—one a conductor, one a uniformed policeman—and there was Roger with Sadie and Berkely behind him yelling and pointing.

Boone opened the back door of the cab and stuck his head above it. He yelled at Roger and waved an arm. He saw Roger coming toward them, faster than he thought he could go with his metal leg. Roger came up to the back door of the cab behind the driver and said, "Get going, we're in a hurry."

The cab driver said, "No way, man, there's a policeman standing there and I don't know what the hell's going on . . ."

Roger opened the cab driver's door, grabbed the cab driver by his arm and jerked him out of the cab. He got in and slammed the door while the driver was getting up off the street. Roger shifted the car into Drive and sped toward the station. The people exiting the doors scrambled and the policeman and the conductor leaped back. Roger spun the wheel of the cab and with tires squalling, raced away from the station with the engine roaring.

Boone found he was breathing again, but he could barely swallow. Over his shoulder, Roger asked, "Where to, Sir?"

12

TEN MINUTES down the road the baby started crying. Boone searched the bag Roger had taken from Sadie, but he found no clean bottles, no formula, no baby food. Only one soiled diaper.

"We need to stop at a store and get some food and stuff for the baby," he told Roger. Baby John's cries were getting louder. The cab raced along an asphalt road that had no centerline markings and the roadsides in the headlights as they whipped by were grown up in weeds and brush. Roger said, "I think there's a town coming up, but don't know about a store open this time of night."

Boone put a hand on the baby's forehead. "He feels hot. We really need to get something for him to drink."

Several miles further on, one storefront behind two antique gas pumps showed a light inside. Roger pulled around to the side, backed up and headed the taxi back into the street.

"Be quick," he told Boone.

An elderly woman wielding a broom watched him come in carrying the baby. The crying had stopped, but the baby was fidgety. In the lights of the store Boone saw how red

Baby John's face looked and he worried about it and what he should do.

The woman said, "He hungry?" looking at Baby John.

"Yes, m'am. We need to get him home to his momma, but we run out of anything for him to drink."

"Looks to me like he's running a fever." She placed a large, wrinkled hand on the baby's forehead. He recoiled and whimpered. The woman said, "I got some baby aspirin back here. Let's give him some of that."

Boone followed her to a shelf in the back where she had a small cluster of infant supplies. The woman worked at the top of the bottle that said BAYER on the side with an image of a baby She removed the top of the bottle that housed a rubber bulb. She stuck the tube from the bottle in the baby's mouth and he began sucking eagerly on it.

"I'd say he's hungry, too," the woman said. "When's the last time he was fed?"

"I'm not sure," Boone said. "We just picked him up to take him to his mother."

"He's on solids ain't he?"

"Yes m'am."

She worked the top off a Gerber's jar and walked with it to a microwave behind a snack bar. She popped the jar in the microwave, turned it on, then went back to the shelf of baby needs and brought back a bottle of apple juice.

"Is he drinking from a glass?"

"Uh, well, sometimes."

"Get him off the bottle, that's my advice. Here, open this bottle and help him drink."

Boone followed her instructions and slowly Baby John

took down some apple juice. While the woman was feeding the baby some mashed-up, gooey-looking peas as Boone held him, Roger came through the front door.

"We need to be going, Bud," he told Boone.

"Which way you all headed?" from the woman.

"Columbia," Roger said quickly.

"Well, you better get this baby into the emergency ward tonight. He's starting to get colicky. You get that started and he'll be real sick."

"Yes m'am, we will," Boone said.

Roger gathered up some chips, put two Landshire sandwiches in the microwave, turned it on, tossed a couple Hershey bars on the counter along with the chips and took his debit card out of his pocket.

The woman handed the half-empty jar of baby food to Boone and went behind the counter. She did some totaling on the cash register and announced a figure to Roger. He handed her the card. After she processed his card and handed him the receipt, he said, looking at it, "I'll be damned. Got more money left than I realized."

"Always a good thing," the woman said.

Roger said to Boone, "Come on good buddy, time to hit the road."

The woman went back to the shelf of supplies and put a package of diapers, another bottle of apple juice and another jar of food in a bag and handed it to Boone. "Figured you'd need this before you got to Columbia."

"Thanks for your help, m'am," Boone told her.

"Don't you go to forgetting to take that baby in soon's you get him back to his momma. She'll know. Don't go to letting him get colicky on you. Babies get colicky and you got a problem on your hands."

In the car Roger said, "Nosey old biddy wasn't she?"

That wasn't the way Boone saw it. Big doubts about taking Baby John welled up inside him. The woman served to let him know how much the baby needed the knowing care of a mother. If Boone hadn't taken his impulsive—and what was beginning to lean toward selfish—action, Baby John would be comfortably asleep in a nice crib in Iowa.

And Boone would be lying in a cold bed with cold thoughts running through his mind, alone, the way it felt to him he had been for the full sixteen years of his life.

13

THEY DIDN'T go to Columbia. Roger drove to the Extended Stay motel, rented a room for a month, asked for a baby crib to be brought in and, after leading Boone and the baby into the room, drove the cab to the WalMart parking lot and left it, taking a taxi back to the motel.

Boone was curious and asked Roger why he hadn't rented a room before if he had enough money to live in a motel.

"Better class of people under the bridge," he said, pointing to the sleeping baby in his crib. "He wakes up still hot and feverish, we'll take him into the ER."

"Yeah," Boone said. What was colicky? He worried about it, remembering what the woman in the store had said. He sat on the bed and turned on the TV and stared at the screen, people moving, people talking. When Roger returned from a trip to the bathroom, Boone said, "I shouldn't have taken him. Wasn't fair to him."

"Hey, the kid's lucky. He's got two daddies and neither one of us is gay."

Boone said, "Do you have children, Roger?"

Roger turned away without an answer, sat, pulled his

pant leg to cover the aluminum leg. Finally, "Had a wife. I came home . . . you remember the famous movie line from the guy, Ronald Reagan playing him, football hero, waking up from an amputation? 'Where's the rest of me?' Well, it wasn't too original, but she borrowed the line.'Where's the rest of you?'"

Boone turned his attention back to the television, tried to picture what Roger had just said. Couldn't. Roger watched the screen for a while before saying, "They've got video games on there. Pay per view. Since we have a balance in the bank account, go ahead and play a few games you want. Probably been some time since you've played, right?"

"Yeah. I'm not in a game mood right now. Maybe later."

"I'm headed down to the Office Max, pick up some supplies," Roger said. He paused with the door open. "Get anything for you or Baby John?"

"Got enough until tomorrow," Boone said. "Who knows where we'll be tomorrow."

BOONE WOKE with a start, his mind racing as if his thoughts had a lot of catching up to do. Was this a school day? Were his parents drunk and passed out again? No, wait . . . they were under the bridge . . .no, he was in a bed. Oh, god, the baby. He stumbled out of the bed, half crawled over to the baby crib and started to probe under the blanket to feel the baby searching for body temperature. He found the baby's face, felt the breathing on his hand, stroked the forehead, the cheeks and under the chin. Normal. Everything felt normal. Boone sat back on the floor. His heart beat slowed and his breath came easier. Baby John's fever had broken.

He saw a light under the door to the next room. He saw by the clock that morning was upon them. Roger was sprawled on the floor, his unattached metal leg lying to one side. He had a number of poster board signs scattered across the floor and a marker pen in his hand creating a line of swirling letters on another board. Boone walked up behind him and read the unfinished sign.

THIS PROPERTY WAS STOLEN FROM
DISABLED AND WOUNDED VETERANS

Roger heard Boone moving on the carpet behind him and looked up at him.

"Whatdya think? Check my spelling for me."

"What's going on?"

"I made contact with some of the other vets down at the VA clinic yesterday. We're organizing a protest in front of the building the damn senator stole from us."

"It's kind of out of the main part of town, Roger. How many people you think will notice your protest?"

"Everybody who comes by the capital. The march is going to start down there and once the media and the cameras show up, we'll lead them down to the building. A couple of the guys play some kind of horn and one of them owns a big drum. He can't carry it any more with only one arm, but he's using his little brothers toy wagon to carry it. Gonna make a helluva picture on the front of tomorrow's *Tribune*. And it will sure get the lead at the five o'clock news spot."

Boone looked at the other signs. "You're using the senator's name? Aren't you afraid he might sue you or something?"

"What's he going to get from me? Take my new leg away from me to pay the senator's lawyer? I don't think so."

"Garrett know about this?"

"He will when we get there." He laid aside a fresh sign that read,

> JOIN THE VETS
> JAIL THE SENATOR

"Want to come with us? You and John?"

Boone thought about it. "I don't know." He looked at the baby, sleeping peacefully in his crib. "Maybe."

WEST MAIN'S mid-afternoon traffic spurted along with bleating car horns and a few shouts from open windows at the half dozen sign carrying veterans dressed in army fatigues, one with an artillery helmet, some with patches on their sleeves, Roger in his bermudas showing off his metal leg, another with a folded sleeve over the remainder of an arm that remained in some combat zone.

A small crowd of onlookers gave them spare moments of notice before dismissing them and moving on. Three teenage girls walking by inquired about the purpose of the cluster of men. When Roger explained their goal of exposing the underhanded dealings of another crooked politician, the girls took the signs Roger offered them and joined in the procession. The girls were attractive enough to catch the eye of several young men passing by in front of the capital building and a flirtatious summons enlisted them. The group grew with the addition of two Vietnam and one old WWII vet who pulled his black Montego sedan with a Purple Heart license plate in front of them and motioned for them to follow.

Boone, waiting around the corner near the governor's mansion, saw the sedan-leading column approaching. The fife player and the drummer pulling his instrument in a little red Radio wagon had been joined by a middle-aged black saxophone player who appeared to have been awakened after a late evening performance in the Players' Bar and Grill. Roger marched at the front of the walkers, shouting and pointing at onlookers, inviting them to join "The parade."

Boone turned so that Baby John, sitting in the front-mounted shoulder strapped baby carrier Roger had bought him, could see the action. Boone liked the carrier. It placed the baby facing him and he could look into the brilliant blue eyes of his son and his son could look at him. On the way down to Main Street, Boone noticed that the baby looked at what they passed and he realized that the baby's world was expanding beyond Boone's face.

Roger saw them and yelled for Boone and the baby to join him. So they did. Baby John looked inquisitively at the flute and saxophone players and flinched at each drum beat. When he saw Boone smiling at him, he unscrunched his face. Office workers now spilled out of capital floors to watch and Boone wondered if perhaps the senator him-self—the subject of the protest—might be watching. A string of automobiles stacked up behind them, though an adjoining lane provided the opportunity to pass them by.

As they tromped past the corner of the capital building, Boone saw a face in the gathering sidewalk observers that looked familiar and his breath caught inside with a shudder. A man there watching them looked a lot like Frank Griffin.

Penny's father. Baby John's grandfather. Boone glanced back but the crowd obscured the man he thought he knew. He only hoped—that if it actually had been Frank Griffin—that he had not been recognized.

His thoughts were scrambling as he tried to think what to do. What if it had been Penny's father and what would he do if the man came after them and if he accosted Boone carrying his grandson? With his thoughts whirling, Boone searched the sidewalk for someone following them and then saw another face that he remembered. This one he was sure about because the man wore a dark suit with a white-turned-around collar. Father Pierce.

Boone looked for a way out.

BY NOW probably fifty marchers had accumulated. Roger pulled them off the street in front of the metal building where he and Boone had showered and washed their clothes. A photographer had shown up and had Roger and the other vets, holding aloft their hand-written signs, posed in front of the small sign that identified the building as a warehouse for the Griffin construction company.

Griffin? Penny's father?

Boone knew that Frank Griffin was the owner of a construction company, but he wasn't sure if this was his building. He moved so that he would not appear in any newspaper photographs, then saw the television van and retreated quickly to the rear of the group and around behind an automobile to avoid being seen on TV.

The street became completely blocked and the sound of

an approaching siren moved some of the people over to the curbing. A black and white police cruiser threaded itself through the gathered crowd until reaching the front of the building. Two uniformed policemen exited the cruiser and began telling people to move aside and stop blocking the street. When the numbers of people began filling the grassy spot in front of the building, the policemen yelled they would have to vacate the spot, that it was private property.

The television camera man had a tripod set up and he was peering through his lens at the crowd of protestors all talking and gesturing in a festive mood. The policemen eyed the camera and tried to stay out of any image that might show up on the news hour. A young woman with a microphone in her hand approached Roger and began asking him about the signs being carried and what exactly was being protested. Roger spoke loudly, but eloquently, Boone thought, as the crowd pushed forward to get their faces on the evening news.

The street traffic snarled itself with the police sedans, the television van, the old Purple Heart recipient's Montego, onlookers and the scabby followers dragging behind the protestors. Boone was of a notion to move closer to hear the TV woman and Roger but an approaching siren kept him rooted. The TV cameraman's back was to him, but he would wait to see who was in the siren-blasting vehicle.

Three men with the appearance of importance stepped out of the marked auto which drove into the entry lane to the building, forcing people out of its path. The uniformed man had braids on his jacket and on his cap. Police chief, maybe, Boone thought. Another man, tall, well-dressed with flowing silver hair was giving instructions to the uniformed officer, pointing with outstretched arm at the TV woman who was still engaged with Roger in her on-the-air interview. The other man ducked back into the police car without Boone getting a good look at him. The police chief—if that's who he was—gestured to the woman reporter and she lowered her microphone and gave the chief a questioning look. Boone heard him say she had to vacate the property, that she was trespassing.

"Are you trying to suppress my First Amendment rights?" she asked the chief, thrusting her delicate chin in his direction. The crowd behind her started chanting again, yelling, "Veterans. Veterans. Veterans."

The chief motioned to the two officers who had taken a stand-and-observe attitude on the chief's arrival. "Evict them," he ordered, and they began shoving their way through the gathering toward the woman and Roger. The crowd was reluctant to allow them passage and one of the officers brought a club into view and began nudging people with it. The woman reporter shouted at the camera man, "Get this, get this," and he swung his lens around to the officers. The silver-haired man said something else to the chief and he moved to the camera man and placed a hand over the camera's lens. The photographer pushed forward and Boone saw the flash on his camera blinking several times. The chief was telling the camera man he would have to move to the street, but the camera man stood immobile guarding his equipment against damage.

The woman reporter had become irate. The officer with the club placed his hands on her shoulders in an attempt to move her to the street, but she wasn't having it. She gave the officer a shot on his arm with the microphone and he used the club to knock it from her hands. She began screaming and Roger pushed his way between her and the policeman. The officer attempted to use his club to push Roger to the street, but the crowd had moved in on him and he couldn't raise his hands with the club. The other officer shoved his way toward his partner, now holding a club of his own. Boone saw him swing the club and heard it contact Roger in the neck or his head.

A voice yelled out over the noise of the crowd, "Stop it. Stop it. Don't hit that man. He's a veteran. He's got a plate in his head."

Boone looked in the direction of the voice and saw Garrett pushing forward. Boone was getting forced toward the commotion and Baby John began crying with people bumping into him and his eyes grew larger and agitated. Boone found himself next to the chief's police cruiser just as the back door opened and out stepped the other man who had accompanied the chief and the silver haired man. He stood within inches of Boone, looking him in the face, then turned his eyes on Baby John. Boone recognized Frank Griffin.

The crowd pushed him away and he lost sight of Penny's father, but he heard him saying loudly, "That boy. That boy."

The leverage of Baby John's weight nearly toppled him over, would have except the pressing bodies kept him erect. He felt a hand under his arm and someone pulling him. He stumbled, kept his feet, held onto the baby tightly, then found they were free of the pressing mob of people. He looked to see who had pulled him away from the cluster of protestors and looked into the face of Father Pierce.

"Ready to get out of here and have some breakfast, Tom?"

14

HE DIDN'T say much on the way to the church, nor did Father Pierce. A few light hearted comments about how Baby John seemed to be growing. And—with a smile—so had Tom. Just before reaching the front door of the church, Boone broke his silence: "Most people call me Boone," he said.

Father Pierce went right to work preparing food, breaking eggs, sizzling strips of bacon in a skillet, chatting all the while. He turned on a small television set on the kitchen cabinet top, poured himself a cup of coffee and sat across from Boone after setting a plate of food in front of his guest. Boone shifted Baby John around to one knee, wrapped his left arm around him and began eating with his other hand. The baby watched him chew.

"Tell me about it," Father Pierce said.

Boone shifted the egg and bacon to one jaw, stared at his plate, and said, "Roger was upset that the building the federal government built for veterans was taken over by some senator and his brother-in-law because the senator killed the bill to fund the building by the state."

"Roger? He's the one doing all the talking? Being interviewed?"

Boone nodded. Took another bite, picked up a spoon and dipped it in the semisolid egg yolk and put it in Baby John's mouth. The baby licked the yolk off the spoon and smacked his lips. Boone gave him another taste.

The priest said, "Looks like your nephew will be on solid food before long."

"He's my son," Boone said.

"Ahh, I see."

After a moment of silence, Boone looked at Father Pierce. The priest waited for him to speak.

"I suppose you'll have to call the police, now." Boone said.

"Why's that?"

"Because I kidnapped him."

"Tell me as much as you want to and we'll see if I can help you."

Boone kept feeding Baby John while he ran questions through his mind. Father Pierce said, "Let's see what's happening to Roger," motioning toward the television screen.

The young woman who had been interviewing Roger faced the camera. "The man who was beaten by the police and arrested ended up in the emergency ward at Capital City Hospital. He is Roger DuPrey, a veteran from the Iraq war where he suffered massive head injuries and lost his left leg at the knee. The police beat him with a billy trying to break up the protest which now has shifted to the hospital where you can hear the crowd in the background yelling for justice for Roger DuPrey."

The bite Boone was chewing on lodged in his throat. His fear for Roger landed in his midsection like a blow from a fist. He looked at Father Pierce. "I need to go there. I need to see him."

"He's your uncle?"

"He's my friend."

The woman reporter again: "A search of DuPrey's hotel room showed other people were living with him, perhaps a woman and a baby. Police indicate that DuPrey may have been planning on a violent act based on the material found in his hotel room."

"That's a lie," Boone said to the television. "I was staying with him in the hotel. And Baby John."

He looked at Father Pierce. "Roger was a kind man. All the violence was in his memories. He talked about babies getting killed over there."

The television switched to a commercial as Boone stared at it. Baby John started fussing, wanting more egg yolk. Boone said, "I hope he doesn't die."

"Perhaps we can go see him when this dies down a bit," Father Pierce said.

"I can't go back to the hotel for the baby stuff. They'll be looking for me."

"We'll get more," the Father said. "Shall I warm up some milk and honey for Baby John?"

Boone ran his hand over the baby's head. "He would probably like that. He likes sweet stuff." He was silent for a moment, then, "Takes after his father."

The word "father," describing himself hit Boone like a streak of sunlight from the heavens. For the first time, the revelation of being a father was a curtain dropping from across his mind freeing thoughts and feelings that had been stored there. Tears streamed from his eyes and he couldn't stop them, couldn't hide them. He stared unashamedly at Father Pierce. "I love him," he said, barely able to get the words out of his mouth.

Father Pierce nodded his head and reached across to place his hand on Boone's. "Would you mind if I spoke with God about it?"

Boone shook his head, hugged the baby to him and listened as Father Pierce said words to God as if God was sitting at the table with them. He would not remember all the words, but he did know that the priest asked God to shed his love on Boone and his son.

"I think you would like to get a lot off your mind," Father Pierce said. "I'm a pretty good listener."

So Boone told it all to the priest, even the part about the drinking and the sex with Penny. And about his father and mother who spent Boone's childhood in an alcoholic stupor, ranting at each other and at him. He confessed his fear of becoming addicted like them and his fear of sex and girls in general. Born out of wedlock—using the word bastard—gave him an excuse to pity them their weaknesses. These last weeks taking care of Baby John made him feel years older than his classmates. Going back to school again was no longer an option for him, even though he had reached the point where he could ignore the teasing and being called Poppa or Daddy because now he was so much older and mature than the ones calling him names.

"And the baby's mother?" Father Pierce asked.

Boone shrugged. "I guess I resent her for rejecting her own baby. I don't understand how anyone could do that."

"What do you plan to do next?"

He hugged the baby tighter. "They won't let me keep him, I know that. They won't let my parents keep him, even if they wanted to, which they don't. If I go back they'll take him and send him off to Iowa or someplace that I will never know about. I will never see him again."

Father Pierce was silent, waiting for Boone to finish his thoughts.

"I couldn't stand that."

"You're what? Sixteen? Seventeen?"

"Yeah, sixteen."

"The court could make you a ward of the state."

Boone looked at him. "You mean, they could send me to a foster home?"

"Likely."

"But not in the same home as Baby John."

"Not likely."

"I don't know what to do," Boone admitted.

"Nor do I," Father Pierce said. "But I know someone who does."

Boone raised his eyebrows.

"God knows," the priest finished. "We'll talk with him about it the next couple of days. In the meantime, there's a small room here for altar boys to use. Has a cot, a chair and a bathroom. No crib, but we can improvise. And maybe we can get over to the hospital later this week and check on your friend."

WHEN THE evening edition of the *Tribune* came out, Boone read it eagerly for news about Roger. Enough information was given to assure him that his friend was not dead, only hospitalized for superficial head wounds and scratches. One picture showed the policeman holding Roger with his billy club raised. Roger's metal leg was visible in the picture as was the look of horror on the face of the woman reporter.

The article did say that Roger would be arraigned in court for trespassing, resisting arrest and assault on the police and the senator. Apparently, Roger had broken free of the policeman's grasp and kicked the senator with his metal leg causing "substantial," injuries to the legislator.

Father Pierce excused himself to take care of parishioners and services in the church. When he returned to his small kitchen where he left Boone and Baby John with a sandwich, some chips and a glass of warm chocolate milk for the baby, he carried a supply of diapers and other baby items he thought Boone might need. Boone felt like asking how long he and the Baby would be able to stay with him in the altar boys' room, but didn't. He showed the newspaper article to Father Pierce.

After reading it, Father Pierce said, "Sounds like your friend could use a good lawyer."

"Maybe the VA can find one for him," Boone said. "He gets a lot of help from the VA. Medical-wise, anyway."

Father Pierce said, "I know someone in my parish who might be able to help him. I'll go see her tomorrow. You can come along. Perhaps she can help you and Baby John, also."

15

STACY LASTER walked with a limp, her left knee being a semi-rigid connector between her thigh and calf, causing her to swing the leg outward when she walked. She was not an apparently attractive woman at first glance, not with the scar that ran from the hairline in front of her right ear to the corner of her mouth. That is, until Boone looked in her soft blue eyes and he saw something there that made him decide she was indeed quite good looking.

She looked at the baby with those soft eyes and Boone wondered then why she had become a soldier and why she had ended up in Iraq where she suffered the awful deformities.

Father Pierce introduced them to each other, and with Baby John. He told her about Roger and said about Boone and the baby that he would get to that, they were a separate case. She had seen the news and read the newspaper. She asked Boone questions about Roger that he wasn't able to answer. Never mind, she told him, she could find out. She knew about the senator and the building intended for the veterans.The prosecutors office was the place to go, she said, to check on the charges, then she would go see Roger if he was up to it. If he wanted her to represent him, she would.

"Now about this one," she said, looking at Boone with those soft eyes.

Father Pierce was able to tell her in briefer and more articulate terms than Boone would have been able to.

"It's a bit complicated," she said. She looked at Father Pierce. "I'm less sure about your standing," she said.

He waved a hand. "In good time," he said.

"Will you have to tell the police?" Boone asked.

"I'm going to have to do some research on that. If you're my client, that will have a bearing. Being under age, perhaps only the court could make you my client. But, to answer your question for today, no, I won't have to tell the police. Not today. Tomorrow, we'll see."

"I'd like you to be my lawyer," Boone said.

"Well, then," she said, holding out her hand, "we'll let a handshake be our contract."

Boone took her hand. It was warm, yet firm. "I can't pay you," he said. "Roger doesn't have much money, either."

"For your retainer, if you'll let me hold the baby for five minutes, it's a deal."

Baby John smiled up into her soft blue eyes. "I'm being overpaid," she said.

SPEC 1C STACY LASTER was on record as the first female casualty in the Iraqi theater when the Humvee she was assigned to ran over a metal case in the street and the explosion took the life of the other three occupants of the vehicle and left her bleeding and unconscious. When she finally came out of the coma she was told that she would probably never walk again. They were wrong about her legs and most especially, they were wrong about her determination. She was told she would not be able to enter the University of Missouri Law School, but the experts were wrong again.

Federal Judge Harold Biggman, a professor in one of her courses at the law school and her mentor since the day she told him after one of his lectures that his subject that day did not apply to combat soldiers, looked at her across his desk and told her that she would not be able to represent the sixteen year old boy she had just told him about. In her mind, she knew that he, too, was wrong about her, but didn't tell him so. Also he wasn't told that the boy had confessed to her that he had kidnapped his own son.

She needed a legal thought on the matter so that she could determine what she should do if she was ever facing a judge on the bench with that very same question. Stacy liked to prepare herself for all contingencies. Her law practice was not all she had hoped it would be. For one thing, she barely took in enough money to live on. Too many times she accepted cases on instinct without giving thought to the ability of her clients to pay. She took the case of every veteran who came in her door. She was partial to abused women and abandoned or derelict children who had suffered at the hands of people who should have been caring for them.

None of these classifications of clients were in high income brackets or—in some cases—any income bracket at all.

The boy and his veteran friend were two more of the same.

She chewed the end of her pencil while she thought, while the computer screen focused on NEXUS and while her eyes wandered to the one photograph on her desk. She wouldn't have been able to say why she kept the 5 X 7 of the young man who had been reluctant to accept her physically after her discharge. They had loved each other in Dexter High School and had enlisted in the Army together, vowing to use their service bill of rights to attend the university to-gether. Allen had been assigned to some cushy job at a base in California for his term in the service and had not been able to reconcile Stacy's combat memories and injuries.

Her office was small, even for her one-person law firm. Her diploma and her acceptance to the Missouri Bar Asso-ciation certificate—both for the benefit of prospective clients who expected to see them where they were, on her wall—constituted her only adornments inside the second-floor, over-the-bank, office. One window did look out on the capi-tal dome, a feature that had been worth the extra fifty dollars a month rent over her other choice.

She made notes from NEXUS and saw something there she was quite sure she could use if she came to represent the boy. She had Googled the kidnapped baby in Eldon and found out a great deal of information and probably knew more about the boy's situation than even Boone did.

Then she turned her attention to the veteran. She called a contact in the police department, then the prosecutor's office, piling up notes on the matter. Roger's permission would be required to acquire his medical record from the Harry S Truman Veteran's Hospital. She wrote a list of questions to ask him, then put her material in a briefcase and took a cab to the Capital City Hospital. The image of Roger DuPrey on the internet was likable to her—she'd been afraid it wouldn't be—and she got a bit of personal information about him.

When she told the patrolman at the door of his hospital room that she had been allowed an audience with Roger, the patrolman checked with the headquarters, then let her in the room. She walked to his bedside and looked down at him, his eyes closed, his breathing even. A bandage was wrapped around his head above his eyes. His eyes opened slowly and he looked up at her. She noted the angular face, strong chin and quizzical, but friendly eyes. He had not shaved for several days, the stubble dark and coarse.

"Hello there," he said. She smiled. "You a cop?"

"A couple of friends sent me," she said. He raised his eyebrows. "Name of Boone and John."

He smiled at that. "How are they? They didn't get busted, too, did they?"

"They're fine. They're worried about you."

"Finally, somebody's worried about poor old Roger Du-Prey."

"I'm a lawyer, Stacy Laster, Fourth Armored." She stuck her rigid left leg out from her body and he looked at it. "I got mine in the first Humvee to enter Baghdad. Where'd you get it?"

He pulled the sheet from his stumpy right leg. "Along the Tigress. Ammo cache hidden in a pile of debris we tried to move to get through."

"Hurt didn't it?"

"Sure as hell did."

"Where'd the cop hit you?"

He hesitated. "You say you're a lawyer? Who for, the cop with the billy?"

"For you if you want me. Father Pierce of the Catholic church brought Boone and John to see me. I've been known to take on a few cases involving veterans in this part of the state. So, I told them I would come to see you. See if you wanted me to represent you."

He continued looking at her. Finally, "I see you got over your disabilities and made something out of yourself. I tried that, but I could never get past the day I got it. Things are all messed up in my head. Looks like you got a brain bashing, too."

"Boy friend and I joined together, pledging to get out and get our chance to attend the university. Only, he decided after looking over what was left of me that he would do something else with his life. All the incentive I needed. My senior year I kept hearing about the raw deal the vets were getting when they came back. That was my incentive to go through law school."

"You're smarter than me. And a hell of a lot more coura-geous. If I could get rid of these spells I have, maybe I could do something like that."

"If you want me to represent you, I'll need your permis-sion to go through your medical records. And I have a long list of questions. But don't let me pressure you. I'm pretty green at this law business. You could for sure find someone with more experience. But I can promise that you won't find anyone who will work harder for you or anyone who will come as close to understanding where you're at than I do."

"How many case have you lost?"

"I've had a couple of draws, you could say. But I've never walked out of court with nothing. Neither will you if you want me."

"Did Boone and John like you?"

"Boone did. He wants me to be his attorney. John smiled at me and I cried."

Roger stuck his hand from under the sheet. "That's the best recommendation I've ever heard. You're my mouth-piece."

16

BOONE SAID to Stacy Laster as they waited in the hall-way in front of the courtroom where Roger's arraignment was to be held, "Why did they arrest Roger after beating him with a billy club? I don't understand that."

"Simple. They're hoping that by arresting him and making him look like a criminal, the jury won't award him a big settlement when we sue the city and the state and the senator and your son's grandfather for unlawful force and assault."

"Roger's suing the city?"

"I'll file it after the arraignment."

Boone smiled. "You're a good lawyer, Stacy."

She put a hand on his shoulder. "Thanks, Boone. You had better get on up to the balcony and stay out of sight if you don't want Mister Griffin to see you."

LEAVING BABY JOHN with Father Pierce and his housekeeper, Mrs. Shank, had been difficult for Boone. Not that he worried about either of them kidnapping his son as Berkely and Sadie had. And Father Pierce was a lot more articulate in explaining to the housekeeper, a fiftyish, kindly appearing woman, than Boone would have been.

Still, he felt almost naked without the baby hanging in

front of him. What a turn his life had taken since the day he picked the baby up out of his seat and walked away with him. Almost daily he tried to focus his thoughts on what to do next. He knew he was on a carnival ride that some day had to end. As usual, his thoughts were like walking into a fog, not seeing, not hearing, not knowing which way to turn. Life had always been thus for him. Worry about which parent—or, likely, both—would be drunk. Worry about his lessons and why they were so difficult for him. Worry about the Ritalin he was supposed to be taking, but made him feel different—spacey—and wouldn't let him sleep. But, he didn't bring the pills with him, so he put that worry from his mind.

Officers of the court walk down the aisle and a tall man striding very upright, looking important like the senator had the day of the protest, approached Stacy his right hand outstretched and Boone could hear him from the balcony call her by name and add a comment about welcoming her to the courtroom as if it was her first time. Stacy smiled back and said, "Mister Langston. Still assistant prosecutor I see," which seemed to take some of the starch out of the man.

Boone did not like Mister Langston.

Others filed in including a secretary-recorder who took a seat close to the judge's bench. Though it was Boone's first time in an actual courtroom, he had watched plenty of old reruns of Perry Mason and Matlock. He liked lawyer movies and shows and felt an eagerness to watch a real courtroom drama taking place in person.

The balcony was small with no more than thirty seats in two rows. The front row seats looked over the courtroom and most of audience below. Only the judge's bench and a fenced in area with a dozen chairs—Boone counted them—which he deduced was for the jury and the table where the court recorder sat and one chair on a level with the judge's bench—possibly for witnesses—was visible from the second row in back. For people sitting there, it would be necessary to lean forward to see the two tables where Stacy now sat and the other table where the stuffed shirt Mister Langston and two young people—one male, one female—sat. Boone sat in the front row until he saw two policemen in uniform, the senator and lastly, Mister Griffin enter. Boone leaned away so that none of them could see him.

The courtroom was large and had a lot of exposed wood, the floor, the pews—almost like in the Baptist Church Boone had attended every Sunday for one year when his mother was trying fervently to kick her alcoholism—the judge's bench, the chairs in the jury box and almost everything else in the room except the white plaster walls and the gleaming brass fans and lights on the ceiling. The smell upstairs was a bit stale with a whiff of floor wax and body odor mixed wafting up from below. Boone liked the atmosphere of the courtroom and wondered what it would be like to be a lawyer. With his ADD would he be able to study to be a lawyer?

If not, maybe Baby John would grow up to be a lawyer. Funny that he should, for the first time, think about Baby John growing up. He tried to visualize himself as a father and he vowed to be a good one. Not that his own father wasn't good to him—when he was sober—he just never encouraged Boone to be anything. Baby John would receive plenty of encouragement from Boone. He silently pledged that.

The thought then nearly strangled him that if he was caught with the baby, they would both end up in a courtroom like this one, before a judge who would take Baby John away from him.

Nausea took hold of him and he leaned back further and held his breath and closed his eyes. Maybe Stacy could . . .

A loud voice interrupted his train of ideas and the wave of weakness that was washing over him. Peeking over the railing he saw a policeman who had demanded in a loud voice: "All rise," and everyone stood. Boone stood. He glanced around to make sure he was alone in the balcony. The downstairs part of the courtroom was empty also with the exception of the two policemen, the senator and Mister Griffin along with the others who would be assuming positions of defense and prosecution. The judge came through a door behind the desk in flowing black robe and took a seat at the desk. The policeman announced that something or other circuit court was in session and that the Honorable Sarah Bland was presiding. The judge was younger than Boone expected, a woman about Boone's mother's age. The secretary, who sat in the recorder's place—Boone remembered that from a Matlock episode where Matlock kept going over to the recorder's desk to ask her to repeat some statement.— took a sheaf of papers to the judge's desk and laid them there. The judge lifted a wooden mallet and tapped it lightly on her desktop and announced that some associate court— giving it a number and a title—was now in session. Everyone sat and Boone noticed Frank Griffin looking around inside the courtroom so Boone ducked back out of sight, then took a seat in the back row.

The judge, reading from the sheaf of papers, announced a string of charges against one Roger DuPrey and said that this was a preliminary hearing on the validity of the charges and announced that Stacy Laster would be speaking for Mister DuPrey and that Rowe Langston would be speaking for the county and for the city. The judge looked at Stacy and at Roger and asked Stacy if she was prepared. Stacy replied that she was, adding, "Your honor," just like Perry Mason always did. Rowe Langston announced that he too was prepared, also adding, "Your honor," but seemingly to Boone, without the respect Stacy had expressed.

The judge looked at Rowe Langston and nodded her head. "Mister Langston," she said, and he rose, looked at Stacy and at the others sitting behind him. Boone leaned back so that if Mister Langston happened to also look upstairs he would not be aware that anyone was there.

Boone stayed out of sight, listening to Langston's authoritative voice as he listed in order the same charges against Roger that the judge had listed. He said that Roger had violently attacked the two officers when they tried to remove him from private property before he could damage it. The way he described the affair was not the way Boone remembered it. Langston called the two policemen to the witness stand where they took an oath administered by the secretary-recorder to tell the truth, the whole truth and nothing but the truth. Each policeman, when asked by Langston if Roger had attacked them, said yes. Boone was not sure what an arraignment was, but Stacy had told him that nothing had to be proven, only that enough evidence presented to allow the judge to decide if Roger should be put on trial. She declined to question either of the policemen. Mister Griffin was called to testify that he had a lease on the property and that he had not given Roger or anyone else permission to occupy it. Boone wasn't looking at Griffin because he was afraid he might glance upstairs and recognize him. He peeked carefully over the railing and saw Mister Griffin rise from the witness chair and start toward his seat with the senator and the two policemen. Stacy told the judge that she had some questions for Mister Griffin and Boone saw him hesitate. The judge told him that she had not excused him and asked him to return to the witness chair. Boone ducked below the railing again.

Stacy asked Griffin who owned the property in question. He said that it was owned by Senator Holmes. "Any relation?" Stacy asked.

"Brother-in-law."

"What was the intention of the building when it was built?"

Langston's voice, "Objection, your honor. Immaterial."

Stacy: "I'll show that if the court insists."

"Certainly," from the judge.

"Why was the building you are leasing from your brother-in-law built?" Stacy again.

A pause. Griffin said, "You would have to ask the owner."

"You don't know?"

"I've heard it was for use by the government."

"The federal government built it, wasn't that right?"

"Yes, so I've heard." Boone peeking over the railing saw Griffin turn toward the judge. "Judge, I don't have accurate information on this subject."

The judge replied, "Just answer the question. If you don't know the answer, say so."

Stacy: "And the government built the building in question, the building you have a lease on from your brother-in-law Senator Holmes, for the purpose announced in the *Jefferson City News-Tribune* as a facility for housing and use by veterans of the armed service of the United States. Isn't that correct?"

"I'm not sure . . ."

Did you read that in the *News-Tribune*?"

"I think I remember that I did."

"So a correct answer to my question would be that you knew before you leased the building from your brother-in-law, Senator Holmes, that the building was built and paid for by the United States Government for the express use by veterans of the United States Armed Services."

"Yes."

"But it wasn't used for that purpose, was it?"

"Not that I'm aware of."

"Why wasn't it ever used by the veterans, Mister Griffin?"

Boone caught Langston rising from his seat. "Your Honor, I see no reason for this line of questioning. The purpose of this arraignment is to determine if there is sufficient cause to bring charges in a court of law against the accused."

The judge, looking at Langston, said, "I'm quite aware of the purpose of an arraignment, Mister Langston."

To Stacy, the judge said, "You're offering this information to the court for what reason? Are you implying that your client was not trespassing because it was on government property?"

"I want it as a matter of record. A record that is open to the public so that anyone who wants to know the purpose of my client's actions on this property will know the truth, the whole truth and nothing but the truth about the complete history of this building."

The judge said, "It seems to me this information—relevant as it may be—would be testimony that would belong in a trial proceeding."

"I don't intend for there to be a trial proceeding, your honor. That's why I'm bringing it up here for the record before I ask you to dismiss the charges against my client."

Langston was again on his feet, "Your Honor . . ."

"I'm going to allow Miss Laster to proceed."

Langston sat down.

Stacy now stood in front of Griffin, but Boone couldn't see his face. "Now, Mister Griffin, lets get on with the reason why this building, built by the United States Government with taxpayers' money for the benefit and use of returning servicemen and women of the United States Armed Services was never used for that purpose."

"I don't know that for sure."

"Well, you must have wanted to know for sure before you leased this building from your brother-in-law why such a building wasn't put to the use the government intended. How were you to know it was owned by your brother-in-law? How were you sure that it wasn't still owned by the government and they might come in and put you out?"

"Well, I knew it wasn't owned by the government."

"How did you know that?"

"The senator told me."

"Did he tell you why the government no longer owned the building?"

"Because he purchased it from the government."

"And did he tell you why it was for sale by the government?"

"The state was supposed to furnish the building and maintain it. But the state lacked the funds to do that."

"You mean the funds were not included in the state budget?"

"That's correct."

"And the states budget is set by the legislature and passed on to the senate appropriation committee, correct."

"I'm not sure . . ."

"And Senator Holmes was chairman of the Senate Appropriation Committee, was he not?"

"I'm not all that familiar with . . ."

"But you know that he was the chairman that year because he told you he was, did he not?"

"As I recall . . ."

Langston: "Your Honor . . ."

Judge Bland said, "Let's finish this, Miss Laster."

"I'm finished, Your Honor," from Stacy.

The judge told Griffin he could leave the witness chair. Langston rose to proclaim that Miss Laster had extended the arraignment with information having nothing to do with whether or not the accused should be put on trial. He said that testimony from the officers of the Jefferson City Police Department could hardly be disputed by the matter of how

Mister Griffin came to lease the building. He stated that he was through, that truthful testimony of the officers established the facts of trespassing and assault and he had no more testimony for the arraignment.

The judge told Stacy she was ready to hear from the accused. Stacy called Richard Drew and when a young man walked forward and sat in the witness chair, Boone recognized him as the camera man who had been present when Roger's protest reached Griffin's building. In answer to Stacy's questions about having a video of the encounter between Roger and the policemen, he replied that he had an extensive video taken that day and that he had brought it to the court. The bailiff who had asked everyone to rise for the judge's entrance helped Drew set up a screen that the video could be displayed on. The judge dismissed several complaints by Langston and soon the room was darkened and the video began playing on the screen.

Boone watched it intently as it provided a better view of what occurred than he had been able to view from behind the crowd. The beating that one of the policemen gave Roger was the highlight of the video. The only time Roger had come into contact with either of the officers had been twice when he had been shoved off balance and his metal leg had bounced off one of the officer's shin causing him to jump back. To Boone, the whole thing clearly showed that Roger had not attacked the policemen, but one of them had hit Roger at least twice with his club, once on the shoulder and once on the side of his head above his ear.

When the video ended, the courtroom was quiet. Langston was conferring with the policemen and the senator, leaning over them speaking quietly, gesturing with his hands.

The judge asked Langston if he wanted to question Richard Drew. He declined.

The judge told him that in viewing the video she saw nothing to indicate that the accused had performed any aggressive attitude toward the officers. When asked if the prosecution had any further testimony to offer, Langston replied that he did not. The judge said she was dismissing any assault charges against the accused, but the video did show clearly that Roger was on Mister Griffin's property. Boone thought she had a tone of warning in her voice when she asked Langston if the property owners were willing to pursue the trespassing charge. Boone understood then why Stacy had gone through the questions with Griffin about the purpose of the building and why the veterans never got the use of it.

Langston said the property owners did not wish to pursue the trespassing charge.

The judge tapped her desk lightly with her mallet and announced all charges against the accused, Roger DuPrey, dismissed by the court.

Boone was so elated by that he almost stood up and clapped his hands. He looked around and saw an older man sitting just inside the open door to the balcony. The man smiled at Boone and said, "Nailed him, didn't she?"

17

A CELEBRATION took place around the table in Father Pierce's small kitchen. Stacy was there, Roger was there, Mrs. Shank stood behind Boone with a hand on his shoulder and her eyes on Baby John who watched Boone's face alertly, sitting without support on Boone's knee. Father Pierce filled coffee cups and hot chocolate cups and placed a plate of warm chocolate chip cookies on the table, announcing that he hadn't baked them, that honor went to Mrs. Shank. She smiled and said it was nothing. She always tried to bake at least one batch a week for her grandkids, tightening her grip on Boone's shoulder saying that.

"Tell us, Boone, about the trial. I'm anxious to hear about if from your perspective," Father Pierce said.

"Better than Perry Mason or Matlock," Boone said. "Stacy's the best lawyer I ever saw."

Stacy joined in the laughter and asked Boone how many trials he had watched.

"Hundreds," he said. "All on TV, of course."

Roger said, "Brilliant how you got that in about the building. Sure scared them off from pressing the trespassing charges. No way the senator wanted that to get in the *Tribune* about the building."

"So you're free of all charges?" Father Pierce said to Roger.

Roger looked at Stacy who grinned at him and nodded her head. "Thanks to an astounding defense by my counsel, I'm a free man. What's more, we made the evening news, I got interviewed by a pretty lady reporter and got my picture in the *Tribune*. I would say we had a very productive demonstration."

"And what's the latest on Boone and Baby John's situation?" Father Pierce asked. "How much longer will I be able to harbor a hardened criminal in the sanctuary?"

"I'm working on that," Stacy said. She looked at Boone. "I'm going to need your parents to sign a contract making me your legal representative. Will that be a problem?"

Baby John let out a squeal as if he was the one to provide an answer. Everyone laughed at him and he joined in the laughter. Boone said, "I tried calling them yesterday and was told the phone was not a working number. I guess they've moved and I don't know where they are."

"Give me their names and I'll get to work on it," Stacy said. But the jovial feeling he had experienced was gone just like that. And Baby John stopped laughing.

As if he knew he had only a week left to live with his father.

THEY WERE back in the Extended Stay room Roger had paid for. Baby John seemed to be glad to be back in his crib and fell asleep right away. Roger paced back and forth in the room, holding the *Tribune* in his hands and talking nonstop about the article and the pictures on the protest march. He proclaimed admiration for all the excellent coverage, the crisp, sharp photos of the policeman bringing the club down on his head, then veered off into criticism about not enough coverage on the veteran angle and the building and how he could be living there right now with others who had returned from Iraq and Afghanistan.

Boone was nervous and irritable. The thought of Stacy finding his parents wriggled through his mind like a black-snake. He wasn't sure he wanted to see them again. For sure they would tell him he had to take Baby John back to his mother. The mother who had given him away.

He felt as he often had in school when his assignments had piled up on him and he didn't know where to start taking care of them. He wished Roger would be quiet for a while. Boone could go for a walk, but, no, he couldn't leave Baby John. And the guilt for taking the baby and for even thinking he could take care of a baby not yet walking struck Boone as being immature and irrational. He tried to think ahead, to picture him walking down the street holding the hand of a child wholly dependent on him for support. Where could he go to get a job? McDonalds? And who would take care of the baby while he flipped hamburgers at minimum wage. His thoughts flew from one crisis to another. He even wished he had brought the Ritalin tablets with him. If only Roger would shut up, just for one minute. Then he realized that Roger was no longer talking. Boone looked around for him and saw him stretched out on the bed, still grasping the *News-Tribune* in one hand. Boone walked to the bedside and looked at Roger who stared blankly at the ceiling.

"Roger?" softly.

No response.

"Roger?" Louder.

Boone touched him on the shoulder and Roger jerked his arm up to grasp Boone's shirt front. His eyes were glazed and looked unfocused. Boone pulled his shirt free and called his friend's name again. Roger sat straight up on the bed looking bewildered.

"What's going on?" he asked, not looking at Boone.

"You okay?" Boone asked.

Roger bent over and wrapped his hands around his face, then began rubbing his head vigorously.

"Roger?"

"It's happening again," Roger said. "What the hell's wrong with me?"

"Should I call somebody?" Boone asked.

No response.

Baby John began whimpering in his crib. Probably needed a diaper change. Boone started toward the crib and Roger said, "Call my lawyer."

"Stacy?"

No response. Baby John's whimpers turned into a cry. The telephone to the room started ringing and Roger repeated over and over, "Call my lawyer."

Boone picked Baby John up from his crib, felt his wet diapers and went to the red Target basket where he kept replacements while the phone continued to ring. Roger lay back on the bed, dropped the newspaper on the floor and swung the hand that had held it to his forehead and covered his eyes.

"Is my lawyer here, yet?"

Boone picked up the phone and heard a man tell him that their rent was due. That if they didn't pay by three o'clock they would have to leave. Boone looked at the clock. 2:48.

A louder cry from Baby John.

Boone sat in the chair, the baby's wet diaper soaking into his jeans. He didn't know what to do.

STACY WAS there. She held Baby John and got him to stop crying. Roger was lying on the bed, his eyes covered. Stacy told Boone to get Roger's things together that she needed to take him to the veteran's hospital. While Boone was doing that he asked her what was wrong with Roger. She said some initials to him that didn't really mean anything, but he thought it was the same thing Roger had already told him that the hospital said was his problem.

"I read his medical history," she said. "I was diagnosed with the same ailment. Caused from shock. I get some weird stuff cramming my brain sometimes, too. They can help him at the hospital, but according to their report, he pretty much refuses treatment and several times he has walked out of the hospital without being discharged."

"I want him to get well," Boone said.

"So do I. The hit on the head the policeman gave him didn't help much. Help me convince him to stay in the hospital for a while."

Boone didn't answer for a minute. His thoughts went to going back under the bridge, but the weather was getting cooler at nights now and that wouldn't be good for the baby.

He looked at Baby John sitting now on Stacy's lap and sucking on the bottle she held for him.

"I want Roger to get well," he repeated, "and I know it's going to sound selfish, but he paid for the room. I don't have any money. They said if we didn't pay again by three o'clock we had to leave and it's four o'clock now." With a shaky voice he added, "I don't know what to do, Stacy."

"I know, don't worry about Baby John, here, we'll figure out something. How was Roger paying for the room? Credit card?"

"Debit card, but he tried to get money at the ATM yesterday with it and he said he only had fourteen dollars and some cents in his bank account."

"Okay, we'll manage. Get your stuff together, too. You can stay at my place for a couple of days until I locate your parents."

Boone took all their belongings down to Stacy's Dodge Ram truck, telling the man at the desk on the way out that they wouldn't be staying any longer. The man told him about the legal checkout time, still talking in a haranguing tone as Boone went up the stairs two at a time.

He held Baby John while Stacy pulled Roger off the bed and stood him up.

"Come on soldier, get your butt moving, here. We've got some places to go and things to do."

Roger looked somewhat bewildered, looking at Stacy as if he didn't know who she was.

"March now, that's an order," she snapped in military precision. Roger wanted to know where they were going.

"We're marching to the vets hospital, now get moving."

"No, I'm not going there," he said, shaking his head.

"That's an order. Now move it."

"Wait," he said. "Wait. I'm a sergeant, who are you."

"Lieutenant Laster," she said. "Now move out."

"I thought you said you were a spec one C?"

"So, you know who I am."

"You're my lawyer."

"That's right. And you owe me money."

"I'll pay you, first of the month."

"Until then, you do what I tell you. Get going."

Boone followed them down the stairs holding Baby John. He marveled how Stacy managed to lead Roger with his metal leg and her with a stiff leg, but she did. Boone got in the back seat of the truck and when she had sat Roger in the passenger seat and buckled him in, then got in the driver's seat and started down the street, she told Boone she had purchased the truck because it gave her more room in front with her leg.

"I'm taking you by my house," she said. "Can't take the baby to the hospital. You make yourself at home. If you or Baby John get sleepy, the sofa makes into a bed. Look around you'll find everything you need. Food in the fridge if you get hungry. Do you have a cell phone?"

"No."

"All right, I'll give you mine. No phone in my home. I'll be back before morning."

18

BOONE WOKE with a start. He sat up, reached his hand out for Baby John and, on not finding him lying beside him, panicked. He looked around, trying to remember where he was. Under the bridge? In the Extended Stay room? At home in Eldon?

He saw the flat screen TV across the room. He saw a recliner with pillows on it. Then he remembered, he'd gone to sleep on Stacy's sofa. He had lain Baby John beside him, on two pillows and Boone had awakened several times during the night, feeling for the baby, afraid he might roll over on Baby John in his sleep and smother him.

He leaped off the sofa and went to the recliner where he found the baby lying on his back toying with the corners of his blanket and making gooing sounds. He knelt beside the recliner and put his hand on the baby. The small, sparkling blue eyes turned to him and the mouth turned into a huge smile.

"Hi, John," Boone said. "How did you get over here? Did you walk over here? And I didn't even know you could walk?"

He lifted the gurgling baby from his make-shift crib that Stacy must have made sometime during the night, felt the wet diapers and Baby John's slobber indicated he could use something to eat.

Stacy didn't respond when he called her name so he looked for and found the dry diapers where he had left them and rectified the diaper situation. In the hallway past the bathroom he called Stacy again. Inside the room he saw the bed perfectly made and concluded she had left her house for her office. Or maybe back to the veterans' hospital.

Walking past the sofa he saw a paper on the floor, picked it up and read a note from her. She told him that she had brought some food for the baby, look in the kitchen, then call her at the office. "Just tell the phone to call the office."

He found the food, fed the baby, ate some cereal, then sat the baby on the floor and, using Stacy's phone, told it to call the office. Baby John tumbled over sideways on the floor, rolled to his stomach, pushed to his hands and knees and crawled to where Boone stood.

When Stacy answered he said, "Guess what, Baby John just crawled across the floor to me. Pretty soon he'll be walking down the street with me."

"ROGER'S NOT doing well," she said. "By the time I got to the hospital he was pretty much out of it. I called the hospital this morning and he's in and out of consciousness. We need to go see him this afternoon."

"Yeah," Boone said. "I want to see him. Maybe I can leave Baby John . . ."

"I've got that covered. Called Father Pierce. It's okay. He'll contact Mrs. Shank. I'll be back to the house at three o'clock. I've got an appointment then, but I called and re-scheduled. Got to be in court at one, but shouldn't be any problem. Be ready at three. Feel free to use the shower."

Boone got the message, he needed a shower. The thought and worry about Roger never left his mind, not even as he played in the tub with the baby. Somehow, although he recognized how crazy it seemed, he thought about the future and spending it with Roger. In a way, he felt he was someone who could help Roger and he knew that Roger could help him. He tried to factor Stacy into the equation, but wasn't sure what would happen when he was found with the baby. He had a guilty feeling that he was imposing on both her and Father Pierce. Now that they both knew he had kidnapped Baby John, they had a responsibility to report that fact to the law.

He was waiting with a grocery bag packed with baby necessities when Stacy got to the house at two thirty. Father Pierce was not visible when they got to the rectory. Mrs. Shank was all smiles as she took Baby John from Boone. John stared intently into her face and matched her smile with his own. If she knew he was a kidnapped baby, it didn't dampen her enthusiasm toward him.

Stacy asked a few questions about the house and how the baby slept in the bed she had fabricated for him when she had returned about two am from the hospital. Boone half listened, they were crossing the bridge where he had started his escapade and he wondered who if anyone slept under there now. The wide river below—he knew it was the Missouri—reminded him once again of Roger's remark about being a pirate on a boat on the river and going all the way to

New Orleans. If they had done that, Roger wouldn't have followed through on his protest march and the policeman wouldn't have bashed him in the head.

"Do you think the policeman's club did this to Roger?" he asked Stacy.

"That's what my lawsuit will say. Of course, the beating he took in Iraq didn't help."

"What will happen in the law suit?"

"We go before a judge and a jury—the jury's important, we've got to request a jury—and we make the case that Roger's a wounded veteran who left his leg in Iraq for his government, then he comes home and the government closes the building that was supposed to be for him and other veterans and sells it for a loss to a politician. Roger spends his nights under a bridge, then decides he will protest what has happened to him and others when the building was closed to him and the police beat him for it."

"I think I read or remembered the teacher maybe reading to us that you can't sue the government without their permission."

"That's true to a certain extent. The city has an ordinance protecting city employees against liability. But, it's not all encompassing. They also, just in case, have liability insurance."

"Do you think you can win?"

"The suit's for five million dollars. Probably won't get that much. Maybe a few hundred thousand. If he comes out of the hospital all right, it will help him get a place to live and provide some living expenses for him."

"You got hurt, just like Roger. Are you going to sue the

government because of the injuries you got in Iraq?"

She laughed. "No. I knew what I was in for, what could happen to me. Can't sue the government over that. I had some insurance against death or injury and it helped me through college."

"Do you think Roger will ever be able to do what you did?"

She waited a while before answering, "No, I don't think so, Boone. Roger's injuries are not the kind you get over so easily. Hope I'm wrong, though."

"What will happen to him?"

Another wait. "He's going to need someone to take care of him."

Boone said, "I want to be that person."

ROGER KNEW them. He was the old Roger for a while, then he drifted off into incoherency. While alert, he had not remembered the protest march nor the hearing before Judge Bland. Roger's doctor came into the room and spoke with Stacy and looked at Boone. Stacy asked about tests and examinations the doctor had made since she had brought Roger in the night before.

The doctor went through a lengthy description of Roger's condition, what x-rays and MRI's indicated and a whole lot more Boone didn't understand. Stacy kept nodding to the doctor and asking more questions and the doctor looked at Boone and said, "You're a relative?"

"Friend," Stacy said.

Boone asked if Roger was going to be all right and if so

how much longer would he have to be in the hospital.

The doctor shrugged and gave an evasive answer, then left the room. Boone asked Stacy, "What did he say?"

Stacy looked at him straight on. "It's going to take some time. Maybe a long time."

"But he'll be all right, won't he?"

Stacy put a hand on Boone's arm. "He says it's fifty-fifty."

"Roger might die?"

"Everybody dies, Boone. Some early, some late."

Boone couldn't speak. Roger dead. He had never thought of that being possible. Stacy said, "Look, lets be up-beat about this. He's resting now, let's look at my iPad. You know how to use an iPad?"

Boone shook his head.

"Okay then. School is starting everywhere, even at your school, I'll bet. What grade should you be in?"

"I finished my sophomore year."

"Let's get you started back to school, then. Let's go on-line and see what you would be studying at your school as a junior."

A list of classes took less than a minute to find. "Look at this, all your junior classes listed right here. Now, the Eldon school doesn't have online classes but some schools do. So let's find one that does and let's get started on your courses."

She executed commands on her computer and soon she had a Third Year English curriculum on the screen.

"While I'm slaving away in the courtroom each day, I'll leave you at the house with Baby John. Only thing you have to do is keep your underwear picked up off the floor, take care of Baby John and study your lessons. Deal?"

"Sure." His heartbeat was increasing as he looked at the words filling the screen on her iPad.

"Okay, Boone, read that first line and tell me what we're going to study today."

The lump in his throat prevented speech. He swallowed, looked at the screen and tried to get the words to unscramble so that he could read them. After a long moment he said, "They said at the school I had something called Attention Deficit Disorder."

"So?"

"I don't know. School is hard for me."

"What are you doing about this Attention Deficit Disorder?"

"They gave me Ritalin tablets."

"Do any good?"

"I can't sleep when I take them. And, my mom says, I get grouchy."

"Ever hear of dyslexia?"

"I think it's where the words are backward."

"That's what I have. Had to cheat to get through high school. Boy friend took the army test first, wrote the answers down for me, then I took it. I had to concentrate really hard when I had to read the instructions on how to man a fifty caliber machine gun. How to read a map. How to remember the parts of an M-4. Life or death. Forces you to concentrate, no more cheating. Same as when I got to college. I didn't just want to pass the tests, I wanted to learn something. It was hard. At times I thought I couldn't do it. Then I looked at my leg and looked in the mirror at the scar on my face and

I knew I didn't have any choice, I could try harder or I could just quit."

Boone's face burned. Stacy might have trouble reading a book, but she could read his mind, he hadn't been trying very hard. He hadn't faced up to the challenge. He had the book he'd taken from the library on how to care for a baby, but reading it had been frustrating, so he had given up on it.

"You told me you would like to be a lawyer like me," Stacy said. "It's going to be hard for you. Almost as hard as it was for me. You still want to be a lawyer?"

Boone nodded his head. He was embarrassed by the tears in his eyes, but Stacy didn't comment on that.

She handed the iPad to him. "Here, then. It's yours. Make me proud."

19

BABY JOHN was growing so rapidly Boone was amazed. Only three days had passed since the little guy had started crawling, now he traveled across Stacy's wooden floors with such speed Boone had to run him down to change his diapers.

He thought about potty training. He Googled it and got some good tips. He dug out the book he'd appropriated from the library and learned more. He stood at the stool and showed John how to do it. John clapped his hands and yelled. After several more attempts, John tried his hand at it and Boone ended up with a mess on the bathroom floor. John ended up laughing.

During nap time, Boone went to a chair by the window and flipped open the iPad to his lessons. The temptation was to look out the window instead of at the screen, but Stacy's words rang loudly in his ears, "Make me proud."

How long could this go on? Life had become too enjoyable, it couldn't last, could it? When Stacy came home from the office at night she told him about her day which greatly interested him. She played with John and like Boone, was delighted with how much he was growing. Boone wanted to ask her about being his lawyer and what was going to happen to him and to his son. He waited for her to talk with him about it, but she never brought it up until one day when she came home early he got his answer. She had located his parents in El Dorado Springs, Missouri and had sent a contract to them to sign allowing her to represent Boone in court.

Fear and dread overtook enjoyable. Somehow he knew it would, everything had been going well, even Roger showed some improvements on their last visit with him. He wanted out of the hospital, of course, but Stacy told him no. She had the military bearing that seemed to strike a tone with him that he didn't resist.

Now his parents would know where he was. And they would tell Frank Griffin. He decided he wanted to talk with Garret so he asked Stacy to take him to the building that was Frank Griffin's warehouse. Garrett would want to know about Roger. Garrett was not at the building, the security man on the job said Garrett no longer worked there. He did have Garrett's address, a small bungalow down by the river with white vinyl siding and a carport. Stacy waited in her truck with Baby John as Boone knocked on the front door, then found the doorbell and rang that. A black woman of medium height answered the door. A small boy about three hung to her dress tail.

"I'm Boone," he said. "Is Garrett home?"

She turned from the door after looking Boone over and said to the room, "Garrett, there's a boy here to see you."

Garrett actually seemed glad to see him and offered his hand. Boone told him about Roger. "Thought you might want to know," he said.

"Thanks." Garrett rubbed his chin. "Sorry to hear that

about old Roger. He's probably going to bust out of there like he did with us." He laughed at that.

"I don't think so this time Garrett," Boone said.

Garrett stepped aside, "Come on in, sit awhile." He looked in the driveway and saw Stacy's truck. "Them your folks? Tell 'em to come inside."

"Well . . .actually, she's my . . .they said at the warehouse you didn't work there anymore."

"Canned me," Garrett said. "Got my application in at the Circle K. Maybe going to work there next week. We'll see."

"What happened?" Boone asked. "I mean, why did they fire you?"

"Well, you know. That day, the police and all. Mister Griffin and the senator, they didn't like it none me trying to stop the police from hitting Roger in the head."

"They fired you for that? And you don't have any money, I mean, you need a job with your child and your wife and all."

Garrett smiled. "I could use a paycheck, that's for sure. We'll make it, don't you worry none."

"I'm sorry about that, Garrett. I know my dad got fired every so often. Had to live on unemployment checks. I know how that goes."

"Don't get no unemployment check."

"Why not? My dad always got one."

"I was fired for cause the senator say."

"What cause?"

"Oh, they say I wasn't doing my job letting you and Roger come in and use the building."

"Oh, no, we got you fired? Jeez, I'm sorry about that,

Garrett. Roger for sure didn't mean for that to happen. I didn't know . . ."

Garrett interrupted him. "They ask about you. Mister Griffin say, 'Who's that boy. Whose baby is that?"

"How did they know about me? About the baby?"

"Video tape. Mister Griffin, he was plenty interested in you. He say, 'I think I know that boy. What's his name?' I said, I don't know his name. So I didn't give you away. You got a history with Mister Griffin?"

Boone was momentarily speechless. "Video tape. So he saw me and Baby John. He's the baby's grandfather."

"I'll be damned. That's what he was so worked up about."

Boone said, "Garrett, do you need a lawyer?"

Garrett laughed. "Me? A lawyer? No, what I need is a job. Why would I need a lawyer?"

"Stacy—that's my friend, she's a lawyer—has a case she let me read about. She's representing someone who was fired—I think they called it prejudicially—and they're asking for their job back or for money."

"Well, I don't think . . ."

"Is it okay if I ask her to come in and talk with you?"

"Sure, you and your friend are welcome in my house, but I don't think I need no lawyer . . ."

Boone was already on the way to the truck. He was back in a minute carrying Baby John with Stacy beside him. He introduced Stacy—Garrett grinned and chucked Baby John under the chin—and inside the house Garrett introduced his wife Jance and his son Dion.

Jance went to the kitchen to fix coffee and Dion ran to

his room to bring some toys he spread on the floor. Boone sat Baby John down to play with Dion and his toys.

Boone told Stacy about Garrett being fired from his job and she asked Garrett questions about it. At the end of the evening, Garrett had promised to visit Roger in the VA hospital and Stacy had promised him she would investigate his case and if she thought he had a grievance she would contact him. Baby John resisted being separated from his first playmate and whimpered as Boone picked him up to leave.

Garrett said, "You take care of Mister Griffin's grandson, now," and laughed. "But you better be on the lookout. My guess is, he's looking all over town for 'That boy and that baby.'"

Another fear for Boone. Another week would pass before Frank Griffin found him.

20

CITY ATTORNEY Rowe Langston's father, Raymond Langston, laid his felt hat on Stacy's desk and sat with a leg-over-knee in her straight-backed client chair.

Looking relaxed.

"I'm very pleased to see you doing so well in your practice, Miz Laster. I've been following you in the courtroom. My congratulations on your success."

Raymond Curtis seemed to be earnest in his complimentary manner. Stacy did not know him well—had only met him once before—and exchanged few words with him. She knew that he had been highly regarded by everyone she had ever heard mention him when he was the city attorney before his son Rowe had been appointed to the job. Rowe, however, was quite another story. Young, impetuous, overbearing were the words used to describe him in Stacy's experience and input from other attorneys.

"Thank you," she told him. "How about a coffee?"

"With pleasure," he told her. Stacy kept a pot on a side table and fixed two cups for them, served her guest and sat back behind her desk. She felt more equal there. That was a thing with her. Maybe because of her injuries or the way she had to scrap so hard to get her degree and how she felt slightly inferior in the presence of other, more experienced attorneys. How she overcame it was to imagine they were seated in a humvee and headed into enemy territory. There she felt, not only their equal, but even superior. She was working on it now, but it was difficult with Raymond Langston because of his standing in and out of the courtrooms and the easy, graceful manner he displayed, putting her more at ease.

"You beat Rowe couple weeks ago on that veteran's march thing," Raymond Langston said. His smile seemed genuine and made Stacy wonder about father and son relationship. "He was right, of course, by the law, I mean. But you nailed him with the video. I was watching from the balcony, you know. Or maybe you don't. Just me and a young boy up there. Who was he?"

Stacy sipped her coffee. "Student maybe. Rowe was tough. I had right on my side."

He continued to grin, then sipped his own coffee. "Coffee always makes me want a cigar, but I wouldn't want to spoil the air in your office."

"Please," Stacy gestured with her hand, "go ahead. Air in here needs something added to it."

Raymond Langston unwrapped a long cigar, offering one to Stacy who declined, and made a production of getting it lit. Through a cloud of blue smoke Stacy asked, "What would you have done if you had been city attorney?"

"Nothing," he said, lightly handling the cigar, then sipping his coffee. "I would never have gone into court against that young man. I know about the building. City got involved. In fact, the city pledged a hundred thousand dollars over a ten year period to the project. But it was ill-founded. The VA never was fully committed to it and the state just log-rolled it out of the budget. Nobody really pushed it after that and the next thing I knew I drove by it one day and saw it was a warehouse."

Cigar and coffee again. "Too bad your boy wasn't around then. Or you, maybe. I know about your military experience. My thanks to both of you for your service. I'm sorry about your injuries. In view of what happened to you, I'm even more impressed by what you've achieved."

Stacy nodded and offered her thanks again. The words that came to her were, "Me thinketh you praise too much," but she didn't voice that to him. His manner seemed sincere, but she was thinking he was softening her up for something. She'd been through this before with other opposing attorneys. Her guard hardened.

"I have a feeling you're getting to the point of your visit, as pleasant and complimentary as it is," she said.

"You're also perceptive. You've filed a case against the city, against the state, State Senator Holmes and Frank Griffin. A pretty big list. You're asking for a lot of money."

Stacy said, "My client is in the Veterans' hospital in Columbia with serious head injuries. His chances of living an ordinary life have been greatly diminished."

"Due mostly, if my information is correct, because of terrible injuries while serving his country in Iraq."

"That's not part of the suit. Neither of us have asked our government for anything for our injuries except fair and adequate care. This case has nothing to do with what happened to him in Iraq."

"But it's going to be difficult to separate the two isn't it?"

She smiled. "We're not going to try our case here in my office are we?"

He smiled back. "No, of course not. I'm just setting up an introduction to the offer the city has authorized me to throw out there."

"I was thinking you were no longer employed with the city."

"True. But, see, it comes out like this. Legally, the city, by their own ordinance, is immune to suits of liability except in extreme cases. Would probably take the supreme court to decide if this suit qualified under those exceptions. So, for practical reasons, time being one of them, that brings in the insurance company. Deep pockets. As skilled as you have become in the legal circles, you might be overmatched by the team of attorneys they would send against you in court. Be a good experience for you. An expensive one, but experience-wise it would be good for you. But, not, I'm afraid, for your client. So, they had a conference. Even called me in. Rowe was dead set against any form of settlement. He had the privilege my position and money afforded him that I'm afraid neither you nor your client had. See, Rowe never saw fit to serve his country in Iraq. Me, I spent some time in Cambodia and unlike you and your client, I came back with limbs sound and unscarred."

Cigar and coffee again.

"So how much you offering us?" Stacy asked, her voice easy and soft, not military.

"The insurance company got up to a hundred thousand

finally after a lot of wrangling. They suggested the city could kick in half of that for them, but Rowe, bless his heart, took umbrage at that."

"Is that your final offer?"

"I didn't want it to sound insulting. I think they are correct in their thinking that they could beat you in court, using your client's battle injuries to their favor. A tactic I personally abhor and said so. Final offer came out to two hundred thousand."

"Quite a comedown from the asking price."

"Five million. Yes it is. Even you would have to admit that's not a figure that is going anyplace."

"That's what the courts are for."

"If you'll excuse me for just one instance of asserting my age and experience into this, I happen to have a bit more of each of those than you and I can say with one hundred percent assurance that no court would ever offer five million for this. Even if your video was in 3D."

"Well, I can be thankful for one thing, that the city sent you instead of Rowe. If he was here and threw a two hundred thousand dollar settlement on my desk I would throw his ass out the door. And I could do it, too."

Raymond Langston chuckled and puffed again on his cigar. "I like you Stacy. May I call you Stacy?"

"Just did."

"You make a good cup of coffee. May I refill? Don't get up, I can do it."

Stacy came around the desk and took his cup. "Wouldn't hear of it."

Behind her desk, she found herself drumming her fingers

on the desktop so she put her hands in her lap. She hoped her eyes weren't twitching as they had the first few times she had appeared in court. Finally she came to the point where she was no longer consumed by fear and had come to conquer her nerves as if seated in a humvee holding an M-4 carbine and surrounded by compatriots headed into enemy territory. Now her realization was that she bore the responsibility for her client's interest, maybe even his life and she did not have the assurance that she held the legal equivalent of an M-4 carbine in her hands.

"Look, Stacy," Raymond Langston said, leaning forward in his chair, "that's the final offer that was given to me. Were I you, I would counter offer a million. I go back with that and after some more wrangling, I possibly get you to three-fifty, maybe even four. Don't bet on that figure, I'm just saying maybe."

"I appreciate your advice, Raymond. Hope I can call you Raymond. Now, here's my final offer. Half a million. We're coming down four and a half million, you're coming up only a half million. Seems reasonable on your part and maybe stupid on our part."

Raymond Langston nodded. Through a cloud of smoke he said, "I'll take that offer to them."

"That's for my client. He's not going to accept that. So let's sweeten the pie for him. Let's add another half million for the project to provide housing for returning veterans who need it."

He chuckled again. "I'll be damned," he said. "You're better than even I said you were." He kept nodding his head and grinning. "That's pretty good. Good PR for them, too.

For both sides. I think I might be able to sell that. Maybe not quite that figure, but something."

He rose, took his hat and held out his hand. "Stacy, a pleasure to get to know you."

"Good luck," she said, taking his offered hand. "Your job's easier than mine. I have to convince my client I'm not selling him out."

21

BOONE AND John were on the floor facing each other, hands and knees supporting them. Boone looked up with a smile as Stacy came through the door, hands and arms loaded with legal material from the office.

"Listen to this, Stacy," Boone said. He faced John again whose blue eyes were locked on Boone's face. "Okay, John, say Da Da. Okay? Da Da. Da Da. Da Da. Come on, say it. Da Da."

Baby John watched Boone's mouth with fascination. He uttered a string of goo sounds and grinned at Boone.

"Maybe it's a bit early for speech, Boone," Stacy said. "Keep trying, though." She deposited her pieces from the office on the desk against the wall, breathed heavily and said, "Guess what. Guess who came to see me today."

Boone stood and scooped Baby John up in his arms. Stacy reached out to rub the baby's head and gave him a kiss on the cheek. "M-I-S-T-E-R Raymond Langston. He used to be the city attorney before retiring and his asshole son got appointed. Seems the city and their insurance company are caught up in a publicity nightmare. The pictures in the *Tribune* must have sent their heads spinning. And then, the video. Just snippets on the evening news, but if the whole 30 minute video made it on the tube, they have too much explaining to do. So, they don't send their cone-headed, idiot son of Raymond's to make us an offer we can't refuse, they send the old Southern gentleman, MISTER Raymond. Anyway, they want to buy us off."

Boone looked puzzled. "They're offering Roger money?"

"Yep. Not the five million I threw up there to scare the pants off them, but seven hundred and fifty thousand dollars."

Boone was stunned. "They're really going to give that much money to Roger? Wow, that's almost a million dollars."

"Five hundred for Roger and two hundred and fifty to the VA project to convert the warehouse to a residence for veterans."

"Really? Really? Man, that's great. They're going to convert the building, too?"

"That's providing I can get the VA involved and get them committed to providing funding for the project."

"But what about Mister Griffin? Would he have to move out?"

"Sure. I talked with the VA today. After Mister Langston came back this afternoon with their counter-counter offer. Senator Holmes will sell the building back to the government for only a hundred thousand dollars more than he paid for it, the crooked bastard. I expect the government can get a better bargain than that."

"So, does Roger know yet?"

"Get ready to drive up to Columbia to tell him."

"Let's call Garrett, see if he would like to go with us. And you can give him the good news about the building. Maybe he can get his job back."

"Already told him. We're going to pick him up in fifteen minutes. Jance and Dion are going to keep Baby John."

Boone watched her search through her papers. When she looked at him and said, "Get ready to go," he said, "I was thinking about taking John with us. I think Roger would like to see him."

Stacy was shaking her head. "Uh uh. No can do. No babies in the hospital."

Boone said, "I've got a plan."

GARRETT LOOKED at Boone standing in the parking lot outside Harry S Truman Veteran's Hospital beside Stacy's Ram truck as he pulled Roger's army raincoat over baby John hanging in his front.

"Man, that ain't going to work," Garrett said, shaking his head. "Not only do you not look like a pregnant woman, you look like a pregnant elephant. They ain't going to believe that."

"So what are they going to do? Arrest me?" Boone asked.

"Okay, I'll go on up first," Stacy said. "You two—or three, maybe—give me five minutes to get Roger prepared for this, then come on up. Don't put up an argument, Boone, if they find the baby and tell you to leave."

Boone looked down inside the front of the oversized raincoat. "Okay, Baby John? You'll be quiet, okay?"

They gave Stacy the time she asked for, then, before starting inside, Boone checked in the mirror, at Stacy's scarf he had tied around his head and at the lipstick she had smeared on him with even Baby John getting a laugh out of it. Garrett, looked at him, smothered a chuckling sound, tried to wipe it off his face, looked at the bulging raincoat with the baby underneath, shook his head and led off for the front entrance to the hospital.

At the revolving door, wide enough for a wheelchair, Garrett dashed ahead of Boone and asked the guard about a wheelchair for his wife. He signed some papers and pushed the chair out through the door, loaded Boone into the contraption and pushed him through the door and on past the guard who barely gave them a look.

In the elevator, four others got in with them and one man bumped against Boone's wheelchair.

"Careful, Sir," Garrett said to the man. "There's a baby inside there."

ROGER APPEARED pale and weak, barely able to lift a hand in greeting. But when Boone pulled off the coat and the scarf from around his head and lifted Baby John out of the carrier and onto Roger's bed, his face lit up and he attempted to rise.

They all laughed at the baby as he bounced up and down on Roger's bed. Roger commented on how much Baby John had grown.

Boone showed him how John had started crawling and told him how he was going to have him talking the next time

Roger saw him. Garrett brought him up to date on the status of the building, which Stacy had already mentioned. When a nurse tried to enter the room to get some vital readings, Stacy blocked her at the door and when the nurse said, "Is that a baby?" Stacy convinced her what she saw was a doll. Reluctantly and unconvinced the nurse departed after sneaking a peek around Stacy at the door.

Boone said, "Hey, Roger, you're a half a millionaire now. What are you going to do with all that money"

"I'll believe it when I see it," Roger said. He looked at Stacy. "Ought to give it to Stacy. She's the one did it."

Stacy said, "The standard fee, Roger. Comes out to twenty thousand."

"Man, you can buy the damn warehouse now, Roger," Garrett said. "No more sleeping under no damn bridge."

"First," Roger said, "I'm buying one of them big Cadillacs. Then me and Boone and Baby John are getting a house of our own."

Boone showed a huge smile. "I'd like that, Roger."

"We'll get us a house looking out on some ocean with a big sandy beach close by."

"You have to go all the way to California to get that house," Garrett said with a laugh.

"Then, that's where we'll go," Roger said. He slowly collapsed back onto his bed. His face was pale now and he coughed for almost a minute.

"We've got to go," Stacy announced. Boone told Roger to hurry up and get out of the hospital so they could get their house. He helped Baby John wave goodbye to Roger and got back into the wheelchair, wrapped the coat around the baby and Garrett pushed him into the hallway. He took one last look at Roger and didn't like Roger's appearance.

Before shutting the door, Stacy lingered, eyeing Roger who motioned her to his bed. She told the others she would catch up and took a chair at Roger's bedside.

"You have the wills all in order, now?" he asked her.

"Yeah, everything just the way you wanted it. After I called you I prepared the document, the one you just signed and the two nurses witnessed. I'll get them filed before the week is over."

"Make it tomorrow," Roger said, his voice barely a whisper.

"Sure. No big hurry, though. The money won't be deposited in your bank account for probably a month. You'll be out by then."

"Make it soon," he said. With a gigantic effort he added, "Just in case."

He handed her a pink slip of paper he had been holding in his hand. "Just one more favor, Stacy. Fill this prescription for me."

She took it, looked at it, then at Roger. "No," she said.

"I need it," he said. "They won't give it to me here."

"Why. Why do you want to do this, Roger? I know what it's for. I know some guys that did it. Solved nothing."

He turned away from her. When he spoke his words were low and faltering. "I can't stop what's in my head, Stacy. Sometimes it stops, then it starts all over again. That's when I know it's never going to stop."

"You have people who love you, Roger. Don't let them down. You think I didn't feel the same way, lying in a hospital, body messed up, head messed up. Could never have a baby of my own. Could never feel beautiful again?"

He looked at her, reached out and touched the scar on her face. "You're beautiful to me, Stacy. If I was going to get out of this joint I'd ask you to marry me."

"Then get yourself able to get out of here. We'll talk about it then."

She laid the prescription slip of paper on his bed. "I watched TV the other night," she said. "That basketball coach was on there, Valvano. Used to coach at North Carolina State. He got cancer and the prognosis wasn't good. They showed what he said to his team. 'Don't give up,' he said. "Don't ever give up'"

"And then he died," Roger said.

22

LINDA BLASINGAME only came in three days a week. Stacy wished it would be more, she needed her five or six days a week, but the money wasn't there. The money on Roger's case would help, but it wasn't here yet. As it was, Linda took home about as much as Stacy did after all the bills were paid. She kept her office door open to watch the small front reception area where Linda sat. She saw the couple come in. They looked lower middle-class—you learned to look for those things with your eye on retainers—the man wearing a suit coat jacket with pants not matching and a plaid shirt buttoned at the neck without a tie. And the dividing line on his forehead between sun exposed and cap-covered indicated he was a laborer. The woman wore an ordinary polyester pant suit that didn't fit well. Her hair was self-styled and probably self-cut and her nails were unpolished.

Stacy walked to the front and greeted them. Something was vaguely familiar about them. The man asked if she was Stacy Laster. She said she was. "We're the Blakelys," the man said.

"You're Boone's parents."

"We got your letter," the woman said and the man glanced at his wife reproachfully as if she wasn't supposed to do the speaking.

"We need an explanation," the man said. "Where is Boone?"

"He's living here in the city now," Stacy said.

"We want to talk with him." The man was stern, but not in a threatening way.

"I'll contact him and have him contact you."

"You know where he is, then."

"It will be up to him on talking with you. Are you going to be here the rest of the day?"

"We have to get back. I only took a few hours off. It's a good drive from El Dorado Springs."

"Please have a seat," Stacy said, indicating the two chairs across from Linda's desk. "I'll see if I can contact Boone."

"He's only sixteen," the woman said. "He's our son."

"I know." The Blakelys had made no move to be seated in the chairs.

"He just up and ran away from home," the mother continued. "He was taking terrible teasing from the kids at school. Is it about the baby? The baby's missing and some people in Eldon think Boone took the baby. He would never do that, I don't understand . . ."

"Why does he need a lawyer," the father asked. "What kind of trouble is he in? Did they find the baby? Is he incarcerated?"

"Boone is fine. He's not incarcerated. He told me he had to leave home. He can be the one to tell you why. He came to me for help. I know that he's underage and that he needs you to agree for me to represent him in court."

"For what?" the mother's voice becoming shriller. "You never said why he's in trouble."

"Let me call him," Stacy said. She picked up the phone on Linda's desk and dialed the number for her cell phone. She heard her ringtones three times before she heard Boone say, "Hello."

"Boone, it's Stacy. Your parents are here in my office. They want to see you and they want to know why you need a lawyer. I'm going to put them on the speaker so you can hear them both."

She pressed the speaker button and, looking at the Blakelys, gestured toward the phone.

"It's Boone," she said.

"Boone?" the mother's shrill voice, "Boone, where are you? What's happening?"

Boone didn't answer for a moment. "I asked Stacy to be my lawyer," he said.

"What do you need a lawyer for?" the father walked closer to the speaker phone and spoke loudly as if he thought he needed to.

"I want to get custody for my son." Boone's voice was weaker than usual. Stacy was regretting she had sent the letter. She should have found a better way around the situation.

"Where is the baby?" the mother was growing louder also. "They claim you took him. He's been kidnapped according to Mister Griffin. He has the sheriff out scouring the whole state looking for that baby. If you took him, Boone, you could be in a lot of trouble . . ."

"You got that baby," the father said, "You better give him back. Griffin says he's going to put you in jail. He says he saw you with the baby."

Boone's voice was breaking, "I need your help. Just sign the paper Stacy sent you. This doesn't have to get you involved."

"We're already involved." The father stared at the phone as if it was Boone. "We had to move out of town to another job or Griffin was going to fire me. He drove down to El Dorado Springs the other day and threatened to have both of us put in jail if that baby isn't returned. I lose this job, I ain't got nothing . . ."

"It's my baby, too," Boone said, his voice crackling with emotion and—Stacy noticed—resolve. "How would you have felt, Dad, if they had come along and took me away from Mom and sent me off to Iowa for some stranger to raise? Would you have cared? Did you ever care about me? Would you have fought for me? Stood up for me?"

The father turned away from the phone, anger strong in his face. The mother was crying big tears and she fumbled in a large, worn purse for a tissue. The phone buzzed indicating Boone had broken the circuit at his end. Stacy put the handset back in place.

"He's got the damn kid, doesn't he?" The father stalked to the door and back. He glared angrily at Stacy. "That's why he wants a lawyer, ain't it? He took the damn kid and Griffin's going to throw him in jail and I'm out of a job." He stalked away from Stacy again, then turned back. He was no longer shouting. "Well, hell, I've been out of a job before. I'll find something. You're the lawyer, are we liable? I mean being the parents and all. I ain't got the money to pay you, for him or for me, so if it's going to cost anything, don't tell me."

"I think what's important here is Boone, isn't it?" Stacy said.

23

BABY JOHN stood erect, two feet down, no one holding him, both hands free in the air straight out for balance, and he stood there for two seconds. Boone applauded him. Then they did it again. And again. When finally Boone let him rest, fed him and put him down for a nap, the longest free-standing had lasted for six seconds. Boone was so proud of him.

He had actually been procrastinating on his lessons to spend time with the baby. Now, he had to get busy with them. As he opened the iPad he could hear Stacy's words once again, inside his head, "Make me proud."

He did some sentences in his English course, typing them out on the iPad screen and sending them to the printer on Stacy's desk. He moved on to American History, linked to Netflix and watched a video on American presidents in the nineteenth century. He found it fascinating. American History was likable and he had no trouble keeping his attention focused on it. Maybe the ADD was going into remission or something.

He went into one of the websites he had found on law. The first part of the description on the site was easy enough even for Boone to understand. He was remembering some of the legal terms and found one section on paralegals and decided he would like to be one and work in Stacy's office helping her with lawsuits like Roger's. He pictured himself walking out of the courtroom after winning a hearing like Stacy won for Roger and pictured himself receiving a seven hundred and fifty thousand dollar settlement for a client.

Yes, he decided, he would start as a paralegal and then become a lawyer. Law firms are named after the lawyers so their law firm could be called The Laster-Blakely Firm. Attorneys at Law. Had a nice ring to it.

The doorbell interrupted his day dream. He walked quickly to the door so that it wouldn't wake Baby John. Probably Stacy would be there with her hands and arms full of papers and needing help getting inside. She'd done that before.

Quickly he pulled the door open and there stood Jack and Twila Blakely.

HE FELT like slamming the door on them, but didn't. Twila tearfully asked him what he was doing running away from home. And why. Then Jack began, asking where was the baby, who was this lawyer woman, where had Frank Griffin seen him with the baby the police were looking for all over the state.

Boone did not explain. His mind was busy accepting the fact that now it was over for him and Baby John. He couldn't breathe, air was not going into his lungs. He wanted Stacy there, needed her there. He saw Frank Griffin coming up the walkway to the front door and anger pushed a fresh supply of air into him and he turned to face his father, anger rising in him.

"You brought him here? What's he doing here? You told him I have the baby?"

Frank Griffin, standing on the step up to the porch where the Blakelys stood, said, "Where's the baby? Let's get this over with."

Boone reached behind him and closed the door. He took Stacy's cell phone from his pocket and told it to call the office. Jack started to push past him, but Boone stood firm. "No one goes in this house," he said. His father gripped Boone's arm, then dropped his hand.

"We don't want any trouble, here," Frank Griffin said. "Let's be sensible about this."

Stacy's voice came through the cell phone. Boone raised it to his mouth, said, "You need to come home," and put it back in his pocket.

Jack said, "Look at all the trouble you've caused for everyone."

Boone heard Baby John whimpering inside. He opened the door, backed into the opening and said, "No one comes inside. If you do, that's breaking the law." He closed the door behind him leaving the others standing outside.

Griffin said, "You'd better do something, Jack. That baby's inside that house. If I have to call the police to get him, I don't see how the two of you stay out of jail along with that delinquent son of yours."

Twila twisted her hands, then gripped her throat. "Jack," she said, her voice squeaky and tight.

Jack Blakely directed his attention to Griffin. He seemed

to be reading his own thoughts and processing them. He said to Griffin, "I don't think so, Frank. That's my son in there and my grandson. And your grandson. We'd better work something out."

"You give me no choice," Griffin announced. He stalked back to his car and drove away.

WHEN STACY got there, Griffin was back with the police. Jack Blakely stood in front of the door, arms folded. The policeman was talking with him. Stacy stepped onto her small entry porch and approached the policeman. "What's going on?" she asked.

"Mister Griffin here says the kidnapped baby is inside. We want to see if that's the case."

"You have a warrant?" she asked.

"My partner is talking to the desk now. He'll find out if we need a warrant."

"You don't think you need a warrant to enter someone's house? That's my house. You can't go in there without a warrant or my permission," Stacy told him.

"If someone's in imminent danger . . ." the policeman said.

"And who is in imminent danger inside my house?"

Griffin said, "That baby in there has been kidnapped. We all know that."

"Can you identify the baby inside the house?" Stacy asked him.

"I remember you," Griffin said. "Rabble-rousing shyster. You think there's more money in this for you? You got a big payout from the city and the insurance company. What more are you after now?"

"What I'm always after Mister Griffin. Justice."

The other policeman came up the walk. He looked at his partner and said, "We need to get a warrant according to the lieutenant. Mister Griffin needs to accompany us downtown to the courthouse. A judge will be there to hear us. The lieutenant says that if the baby is the kidnapped baby, then to arrest the owner of the house and whoever we think has been harboring the kidnapper or kidnappers."

"Okay," Stacy said, "Let's end this the sensible way. I'm calling Child Services. They will take custody of the child." To Griffin she said, "And if we can't work this out peacefully, then you and I will see each other in court again, Mister Griffin."

24

IT WAS over. Whatever "It," had been. Six days had passed since the woman from Child Services had come into Stacy's house and had taken Baby John with her and out of Boone's life. He had heard Stacy in her SPEC 1 C voice demanding a string of concessions from the police and from Frank Griffin. From Jack and Twila Blakely, too. He heard the words, but they had not gone inside his thinking mind. He couldn't recall any of the words. The only thing he understood was that Baby John was gone from his life, perhaps forever, and somehow Stacy had kept him and his parents from being taken into custody by the police.

Small comfort. He did remember his parents—especially his father—telling him he had to go back to El Dorado Springs with them, but again Stacy had intervened. He stayed in her house, trying to sleep, trying to concentrate and lay out a plan for the rest of his life as he had been doing in his plan to become a lawyer, but all inspiration had left him. He was back to being alone, the way he had felt all his life so he shut down his mind and went back to sleep.

Stacy brought her upbeat attitude home with her each evening. She tried to cheer him up. She talked about what she had done in court that day, explaining it to Boone, using the terms he had been remembering from the websites he had been on. He tried his best to concentrate on what she was saying, but to no avail. More than once in the middle of one of her cases he would ask her stuff like: "Where do you think he is? Who has him now? Are they feeding him right? He doesn't like those egg things in a jar."

This evening she was especially ebullient. "Roger got his first check today. A hundred thousand dollars deposited in his bank account. I called him and we're going up there. Order a pizza, have supper with him. Come on."

Roger knew about Baby John. He told Boone he was sorry about it, his voice weak and dragging. At times it seemed as if Roger didn't realize where he was or who they were. As if he was no longer with them. Boone worried. Roger didn't say much about the money. Just, "Okay, that's good." Boone asked if he wanted him to buy something special and bring it to the hospital. Maybe a new gown or how about a pair of sheepskin lined house slippers.

"Look good on your metal foot," Boone told him. Roger only smiled about it. On the way back to Stacy's house, he asked her about it. What were the doctors saying? Would Roger get better?

"It was fifty-fifty," she told him. "It's gone down a little since then."

"What's going to happen to him?"

Stacy waited a time before answering. "I think it's going to take awhile, Boone. Don't expect too much."

Boone finally said, "I'm bad luck. Something bad happens to everyone in my life. Hope nothing bad happens to you."

Smiling over at him she said, "Already has. Something not so good over in Iraq and something good when I met you."

"Humph. Don't be too sure about that."

"I never told you, but when I got my injuries, I came out of it with this leg and scar you can see, but inside I hurt pretty bad too at the time. See, I can't have any children. One of the things drove my fiance off, I guess. So I met you and I consider you the son I could never have."

Boone was surprised at that. He hadn't thought about Stacy as his mom. More like a big sister, maybe. He had realized for the first time what love was with Baby John. His feelings toward Stacy was something like that, only in reverse. With the baby he provided the strength and reliance for him, but with Stacy, he depended on her for the same thing. He didn't know how to respond. He tried humor. "Thanks, Mom."

"I don't mean to take your mother's place, Boone. Stay with me as long as you want. We'll work this out. You're the legitimate father so you have rights. You have standing in court. Baby John is under temporary custody with the State right now, but a custody hearing has to be set. The Griffins have postponed one hearing already. When it happens, we'll be there. You'll have something to say about it. I'm studying case law now to see about similar cases, if there are any."

"What's case law?"

"Like I said, other cases similar to yours that a court has made a ruling on somewhere. You can go in and ask for a ruling like the one that has already been made. Case law has a big influence on judges."

"Where do you find these cases?"

"Go online. Look at West or Nexus. I'll show you how. You can do my research for me. Be good for both of us."

"What would I look for?"

"I'll show you. You can get started tomorrow. Deal?"

"Yeah. I'd like that."

They pulled into her driveway and Stacy shut the engine off in her Ram truck. Boone with his hand on the door handle, froze for a moment.

"Stacy?"

"Yeah, Boone."

"I love you."

THE RESEARCH project returned inspiration to Boone's life. He dove into it with a vengeance. When he had been upbeat about being a lawyer, just before they took Baby John away, he was sure his ADD was gone. That he was normal. After the baby was gone, he felt as he had many times in school, unable to concentrate, disinterested. Now he was energized again. He spent his days searching the legal websites looking for a case of an underage father seeking child custody. He would have several cases to show Stacy each evening and they would research them together. Boone actually began to feel like he was a real paralegal.

Stacy enrolled him in several legal courses online, paying the tuition and fudging some of the prerequisites. Two weeks had lapsed when she told him that a custody hearing had been set three weeks away.

"We need that case law," he said, more determined than

ever in his research. He found something the next day. Cheer and hope returned for the first time since he had watched Baby John being carried out the door. When Stacy returned from work she was greeted at the door with a beaming face.

He showed her the case, a seventeen year old girl had requested in court to be placed under custody of her older brother. The court ruled she had adequate reason to make the request and the brother was qualified to take custody of her. The court granted custody.

"See," he said, his enthusiasm overflowing, "she's the same as me. I could ask for you to take custody of me, then when we go to the hearing for Baby John, I wouldn't just be an under age father, I would have you providing custody for me so I could provide custody for John."

"It's kind of a long shot," she said. "Be worth a try, but John's hearing is only three weeks off. Be hard to get one scheduled for you before that. Court's pretty crowded. They're scheduling six months away."

"But you'll try?"

"That's our best shot. Sometimes custody cases can jump ahead in the line since six months in a baby's life is a long time."

"We can do it, Stacy, I know it."

She had not seen this type of passion in Boone since Baby John had been taken.

"Are you sure about this, Boone? It's like turning your back on your parents."

"Yeah, I know. I've thought about that. They're basically good people. Not very loving and living in a house where the two adults always drunk and yelling at each other is no fun.

But, they would have been ineligible for custody of Baby John, what with their past troubles. Besides, I consider myself an adult now. Just a legalism away."

Stacy laughed at him. "Legalism, huh? You really are getting into this legal thing. Next thing I know you'll be a junior partner."

"What I had in mind," he said seriously.

She was able to get her court date, two days before the custody hearing on Baby John. Her threat to force postponement of that hearing if she couldn't get a date for Boone's hearing helped her onto the fast track. She didn't get the judge she wanted, but she got the date.

Good news to pass on to Boone.

Too bad it wasn't to last.

SHE DIDN'T want to tell him, it would break his heart. Again. He didn't deserve this kind of news. She left the office early and stopped at a small lounge where she knew people from the courthouse met for drinks. The friendly face of a court stenographer at a booth caught her attention and she slid in across from her, asking if it was okay. It was.

She enjoyed small talk and gossip around the courthouse, trying to forget her most pressing thoughts. After two drinks her friend said she had to get home to a husband and kids.

"I forget," she said to Stacy. "Are you married? Kids?

"Neither." Stacy finished her drink and signaled a passing waitress for another. "I have a young boy staying with me. I'm asking for custody with him in a couple of weeks.

But, tonight I don't want to go home. I have some bad news to tell him. And I don't want to tell him."

"Sorry. Anything I could help with?"

"I wish, but no. How do I break bad news to a teenage boy?"

"Buy him a red Mustang," the friend said with a laugh.

As the woman left the booth, Stacy's thought was, "It's worth a shot."

She came through the door dumped the homework she carried with her on the desk and said to Boone, curled up on the sofa with the iPad on his knee, "Come on, hurry up. We've got to get someplace before they close."

Boone slowly closed the iPad and said, "Where we going?"

"It's a surprise. Come on."

Driving down the street Boone was still pumping her for their destination. "You'll see," was her only response. She pulled into the lot in front of the nearest Ford dealership.

"Come on, get out," she said. "Help me pick a car."

"A car? You have a truck."

"I know. I want a car. Pick out the coolest car on the lot for me."

"Really? You closed a big deal today?"

"Never mind. I just want a young guy's idea of the coolest car in town."

The idea was beginning to grow on him. "Okay," he said. "The coolest one, right?"

"Right."

They walked the lot from one end to another. A friendly salesman followed them and Stacy told the young man not to be a pest and it would be worth his time. Boone tried several cars, got inside, tried the seats, adjusted the mirror, then the radio and the GPS. When they got to the last car to be looked at, Stacy asked, "Which one. What's the coolest one on the lot?"

"I like red," Boone said. "The red Mustang would be the coolest one on the lot. Why are you buying the coolest car on the lot?"

"It's for you," she said. She smiled hugely while he digested that.

"Me? You're really buying a car for me? Why?"

"Because you're the coolest guy in town." She let that settle on him for a minute, then, "It's from Roger to you. He wanted me to buy it for you."

He was stunned. Tears came to his eyes and he didn't speak. He turned to his side trying to conceal wiping the tears.

"He got the money, you know," she said. "He wanted to share it with you."

"I don't know what to say," Boone told her. "No one's ever bought anything for me before. Once I wanted a motorcycle, but I outgrew that. Didn't get one, anyway. Wow, a red Mustang. Just for me."

"Yep. Just for you. Want to drive it home? I'll go get it ready and pay for it. Then we're going out to dinner. Best place in town. We can just sit around and talk the rest of the evening."

"Thank you Stacy. We've got to go see Roger so I can thank him, too."

"We'll talk about it," she said. "After dinner."

BOONE TALKED throughout the meal. Stacy was glad to see him finally be the old Boone. The Boone he was before they took Baby John away. He explained everything inside the Mustang to her, told her how it worked. He planned trips with her, how he was going to take Roger with him and maybe the court would let him take Baby John. He followed her truck in his new car, parking beside it in her driveway. He laughed with her about how nervous he was since he had only driven the car in Drivers Ed to get his license and his dad's truck a half dozen times.

Stacy sat beside him on the sofa and let him go on about his new car. When a lapse finally came, when Boone had talked himself out, Stacy said, "The car's a special gift, you know. It's Roger's way of showing his love for you."

"Yeah, you're right. I can't wait to show it to him."

"Everywhere you go in the car, whenever you're sitting in it, whenever you look at it, you'll be able to feel Roger's love for you. Always remember that."

"I will. I know Roger doesn't say much about how he feels, but I know he loves Baby John. And me, too, I'm pretty sure. Well, he bought me a car, that's proof right there."

"Make me a promise. Don't ever forget Roger and the car he gave you."

Boone turned to look at her quizzically. "Well, yeah, sure. Why would I forget?"

Stacy laid a hand on his hand. "Boone, the hospital called this morning. Roger died last night."

25

THE NIGHT finally ended. She had stayed with him, holding him in her arms until he had at last gone to sleep. The weeping was over. The joy he'd known had been sucked out of him. All that happened to him, how was a sixteen year old boy supposed to withstand that?

She'd been through it before. She'd seen the blood of young men spilling onto the streets of Baghdad and she'd known the feeling of learning a friend, barely old enough to shave, dying after the terror of war had torn him apart. She never got used to it. When she lay in the hospital with terrible injuries, she watched the bodies of the young being rolled down the hallways to be shipped back home with no earthly possessions left except a flag draped coffin.

No, death was not something easily accepted. But, death had to be accepted in order to go on living. Boone would go on living with a new hole in his heart. How was she going to be able to help him understand how to do it.

Roger had known he was dying. She wanted to believe, and did, mostly, that he hadn't forced his death, that he hadn't tried to fill the prescription for pills that would have done just that. He had given her specific instructions. He did not want her to try to find a brother he hadn't seen in ten years. Nor a father, if he was still alive. If they found out about the money he'd been awarded, there would be endless court battles with them trying their best to get their share of it. No, he wanted everything to go to Boone and Baby John after a hundred thousand was added to the VA building and fifty thousand to Stacy—twenty more than the bill for her service— and ten thousand to Garrett. He instructed Stacy to set up a trust fund for Boone as he was a minor and he wanted Stacy named as the executor of Boone's trust fund and Roger's estate.

Now she had to prepare his funeral. Roger wanted an extravagant service as a display to the public and to remind them of the veterans in their midst. She wanted Boone to help her make the preparations, thinking it would help him accept the death of his friend.

When Boone woke she talked with him about what they needed to do. She thought he looked older today. Lines bordered his eyes, lines that weren't there yesterday. He talked very little, but he did seem interested in helping her plan the funeral service and the burial. They called Garrett, told him the news, and asked for his help in the planning. Garrett had very little to say except, "Damn, damn, damn."

Stacy made several calls to finally get a space for Roger in the Jefferson City National Cemetery. Boone made calls, as did Garrett, in arranging for a rifle squad, Boone sounding mature. He was even able to arrange a flyover of a bomber from the air base in nearby Knob Noster. Stacy took him to Dillards and purchased a suit, shirt and tie. Boone exhibited a purpose now, a dedication she hadn't observed in him before. He seemed to be growing up right before her eyes.

The day of the funeral dawned bright and sunny with a bit of cool autumn air. They drove to the service in the red Mustang, Boone driving. The *News-Tribune* had carried an article on the front page about Roger's death and about the services for him. The motorcycle group that accompanied burial services for military members led a long parade of traffic to the cemetery and the crowd that gathered near the burial site for Roger was populated by numerous uniforms and VFW and American Legion caps.

Father Pierce, having volunteered to give a graveside prayer, stopped in front of Boone, seated with Stacy at graveside, and told him he would like for Boone to meet Mrs. Allen. A small, middle-aged woman carrying a baby in her arms, was beckoned by Father Pierce. Boone looked up to see Baby John smiling down at him.

Boone could not speak, even as Mrs. Allen handed the baby to him. As Boone kissed him, Baby John's arms went around his neck in a hug. Stacy was the one who shed tears, but emotion could not have been greater in anyone than in Boone. Days and thoughts of doubt were erased. Father Pierce explained that Mrs. Allen had temporary custody of Baby John—awarded by the state until the court hearing on his final custody occurred. Being one of Father Pierce's parishioners, she agreed to bring the baby to the services.

Boone held Baby John tightly as they watched the color guard and the horse-drawn caisson bearing the body of his friend, watched as Garrett in his old uniform with five others in uniform placed the flag covered casket over the open grave. They listened gravely to Father Pierce's spiritual words and he gripped his son closer still as the baby flinched with each shot fired by the rifle detail. Boone pointed out the plane in the sky to Baby John during the flyover. A bugler stepped forward and played Taps. The mournful tones echoing through the acres of upright headstones that marked the final resting places of the hundreds of fallen warriors, off the memorial that memorized the 108 Union soldiers massacred by bushwacker Bloody Bill Anderson at Centralia. The bugler let his final notes fade before he lowered his bright, brass bugle. Baby John sat very still on Boone's lap, turning to look into his face.

Garrett folded the flag on the casket and brought it to Boone who stood, holding the baby in one arm, the other hand accepting the trifolded flag. Garrett, looking at both Boone and Baby John, said, "On behalf of the President of the United States, the United States Army, and a grateful Nation, please accept this flag as a symbol of our appreciation for your loved one's honorable and faithful service."

Boone surrendered his friend to the earth and his son to Mrs. Allen. He put his arm around Stacy and said, "Let's go home."

26

THE DAYS grew long following Roger's funeral. Boone became increasingly silent, keeping to an intense regimen on the computer, studying, vowing to Stacy he was going to get a GED diploma so he could enroll in a university. She thought it would be a good thing for him. That he needed the association of other young people to help him through the events of the last few weeks. He, with the help of Father Pierce, attempted to get some visitation permission from Child Services, but that had not occurred. Boone did get to see Baby John once again when he attended mass at Father Pierce's church on a day Mrs. Allen brought the baby.

The time arrived for Boone's custody hearing. He had become so mature since he lost his son and his friend died that, to Stacy's mind, it seemed absurd to have a hearing about someone taking custody of this boy who had endured more in the last few weeks than some do in a lifetime, and he had now become a young man. She put together the best case she could, not knowing exactly who and what objections might occur.

Being a juvenile case, only persons with standing were allowed in the courtroom. Jack and Twila Blakely were there. Sitting with them was Nelson Gundry, a Kansas City attorney that Stacy knew only by reputation. Gundry, said by others, was a cutthroat lawyer who would sell his services to the devil for pieces of eight. Stacy wondered who was paying him.

The judge, Ann Merrill, had been referred to by other attorneys as "Hard-Assed Annie." She was a harsh-appearing woman with wiry gray hair untamed. Her features were rock-hard with blazing gray, steely eyes. Eyebrows were the most prominent feature of her face, bushy and stiff like wire brushes. Stacy had never been in her court before. She only wished for justice, but she'd been an attorney long enough to know that sometimes justice was nothing more than a wish. But, not always.

Stacy began her opening remarks by citing the case Boone had found online, of the underage girl who appealed to the court of her own accord to be in the custody of her older brother. The first testimony was given by Boone who stated, before the judge, that he wished to be in the custody of Stacy Laster because she was providing assistance and support for him during trying times in his life and that she had been an invaluable source of strength and care during a difficult period that he had not received, nor believed he could receive in the home where he was living with his parents.

"Were your parents abusive toward you?" the judge asked.

"No, your honor," being cautioned by Stacy to show deference and respect to the bench.

"Did they provide sustenance as far as food and shelter and clothing?"

"Yes, your honor."

"Did they deny anything to you that you thought you were entitled to?"

"No, your honor."

The judge said, "I'm not understanding. If your parents provided everything to you that you felt entitled to, explain why you're seeking custody by Mrs. Laster."

"They couldn't deny me what they didn't know about," Boone said, trying not to sound as if he was reading a piece he had actually spent hours remembering. "I have been diagnosed with Attention Deficit Disorder. I had problems with my studies, with school. I was the father of a baby. My days in school became unbearable. My responsibilities changed after that and I wasn't able to adjust. My parents were not able to bear my difficulties nor guide me in adjustment. Stacy was. I went to her when I needed help and she gave it to me. She inspired me to tackle my studies and to conquer my fears and my feelings of inadequacy. She has helped me on the road to furthering my education to become an attorney that helps others. Like she is. I am not turning my back nor rejecting my birth parents, this is a legal matter for me, not an emotional or moral matter. That's why I am here in court, for a legal adjustment."

The judge studied him with a hard gaze, then leaned back in her chair. "I see," she said. She directed her attention to Nelson Gundry. "Mr. Gundry, any questions?"

Gundry stood. He looked as if he had dressed for court in a hurry. His suit was at least one size too small for his short chunky body, his shirt unpressed with one button under his skewed tie missing. His belt was fastened crookedly with one end nearly curling to his knees. His shoes lacked polish, one untied, the laces dragging the floor. He rose slowly from his chair and—as if deciding to battle the judge on her worst feature—his eyebrows shot up and down over dark beady eyes dancing as if looking forward to some great treat.

Boone shrunk back slightly as Gundry approached him. "May I approach the witness, your honor?" he asked as he proceeded to do so before receiving permission from the bench.

"Now tell me Doon, is it Doon?" he asked. Behind him Stacy said, "It's on the paper."

"Oh, yes," pretending to scan the paper, taking a long minute. "Here it is, Boone. Boone Blakely. Right?" Not waiting for an answer, he continued. "And you're wanting to what, become a ward of Miss Stacy . . .let me get it right, here, MISS (with emphasis) Stacy Laster . . ."

"Objection, your honor," from Stacy. "The petition doesn't contain the word ward."

"But that's what it is, isn't it, your honor? She wants to be his guardian . . ."

"Stick to the petition," Stacy said.

Judge Merrill said, "I'll give the instructions here Mrs. Laster."

"I just thought Mr. Gundry needed some help with his legal definitions, your honor."

"Stick to the petition, Mr. Gundry. If it needs rewriting, the court will do it."

"Of course, your honor." Turning back to Boone, "Now then, you are what fifteen? Sixteen?"

"It's on the petition," Stacy said.

"Mrs. Laster, the court will be the one to address counsel regarding the petition."

"This is a serious matter, your honor," Stacy said, "at least it is to everyone here except, it seems, Mr. Gundry. Let him prepare for the proceedings by actually reading the petition and stop trying to play games with Boone Blakely who is here for something of great importance to him."

Judge Merrill placed Gundry in her fixed gaze. "Please assure the bench and Mrs. Laster that you are fully prepared to have this case adjudicated, that you have read the petition and that you will not require any more time to peruse it."

"Oh, absolutely, your honor . . ."

"Then get on with it."

"Yes, m'am, your honor."

Turning back to Boone again, "

"Now, BOONE" (with emphasis) "you're sixteen, according to the petition here, and Miss Laster is twenty-something . . ."

Stacy stood and said firmly, "Thirty-two, it's in the petition."

Judge reached for her mallet and tapped it harshly on her bench. "Counsel will approach the bench."

Stacy walked to the bench while Gundry shuffled forward, looked at Stacy and grinned.

Judge Merrill looked first at Gundry then at Stacy. "That's enough. The court is in recess for ten minutes to allow Mister Gundry to read the petition in it's entirety. When the court reconvenes, if the bench has to re-enter this line of distraction, there will be a contempt citation. Understood?"

Gundry pulled on his gravy-stained tie.

"Yes, your honor."

"We're not here to play games," Stacy said. "Let Mister Gundry try his parlor games elsewhere. The petitioner and the witness is sixteen years old. Stop toying with him."

"I'm still the one to give advice to counsel, Mrs. Laster."

"It's Miss Laster," Stacy said. "It's in the petition." She turned back to her chair and gestured to Boone. "Court's in recess," she told him.

Judge Merrill left the courtroom while Gundry went to his table and proceeded to make a showing of flipping pages in the petition.

Boone stepped down from the witness chair and walked to Stacy's table looking at her in a questioning manner.

Stacy tilted her head in Gundry's direction. "Jerk," she said.

"NOW THEN, Boone, I understand you have had several difficult occurrences in the last few months. That you have had a son taken away from you, a son that you kidnapped from a caretaker without permission and that you have lost an acquaintance lately. Is that true?"

"The baby is my son."

"But no court had ever granted you custody, right?"

"No court has ever refused custody to me."

"All right, we'll take that up later. First, let's talk about this acquaintance you say you had . . ."

"Objection," from Stacy. "There is nothing in the petition about an acquaintance. Let's stick to the facts in the petition."

"Explain, Mister Gundry," from Judge Merrill.

"Happy to, your honor." To Boone, "Roger DuPrey. You were acquainted with him?"

"Yes."

"As was Miss Laster."

"She was his attorney."

"And after he contracted Miss Laster to represent him in an assault case with the city of Jefferson City, She offered to represent you. Correct?"

"Yes."

"And this Roger DuPrey ended up in a scuffle with the police and went to the VA hospital with injuries he had received in Iraq as a soldier and with injuries he said he received at the hands of the Jefferson City police. You don't need to answer unless I'm telling you wrong. And Miss Laster, who is herself a wounded veteran from Iraq, prevailed upon the city to award this Roger DuPrey a total of seven hundred and fifty thousand dollars in a settlement . . ."

"Objection, your honor," from Stacy. "This is a matter Boone Blakely was not involved in and therefore would not necessarily possess the legal interpretation to answer Mister Gundry's questions about the matter."

"Your honor, I just want this as a matter of fact entered into the record. Because, you see, Boone Blakely WAS involved in the case and I'll explain how."

"Then get your facts straight," Stacy said.

The judge tapped her mallet. Gundry shuffled quickly back to his table and picked up a sheaf of papers. "I have the facts, your honor. I'd like to enter them into record here."

"He doesn't have the facts, your honor. If he does have

them, he's in contempt of court. The amount of the settlement is not public information and the case says that. I'd like to see the paper he has and if it's the court record, a record that's been closed to the public, then I would ask the court to find Mister Gundry in contempt."

"Let me see the papers, Mister Gundry," the judge said.

"But, your honor . . ."

The judge extended her hand across the desk. Gundry laid the papers on his desk and shuffled a stack around making a show of it. The judge tapped her mallet again. "*Now*, Mister Gundry. Any and all papers you possess that reference the settlement you spoke of."

"Yes, your honor." He shuffled to the bench and handed her a thick roll of papers. The judge looked at the papers, flipping the sheets, reading, then looking up at Gundry, "Where'd you get this record?"

"From someone involved, your honor. He has a perfect right to have the papers and to divulge the settlement to anyone he chooses."

"From whom did you get the papers. I want a name."

"I'll provide it to the court in a memorandum."

"You'll provide it to me now, Mister Gundry."

"The person who gave them to me was none other than Senator Jess Holmes," Gundry said.

"We'll take that up in a separate manner," the judge said. "Now, continue, and if you use anything else in this report I'll find you in contempt."

"Your honor," Stacy stood, "It's my understanding that one does not get—to use a golfing term—a mulligan when it comes to a contempt charge for divulging a closed record."

"I said we would get to that, MISS Laster." To Gundry, "Let's get on with this. Don't make me remind you to stick with the case at hand again, Mister Gundry."

"Yes, your honor, my apologies to the court."

He walked away from the bench, then knelt to tie the maverick shoe laces. Straightening, he came back to confront Boone quickly. "You're the beneficiary of Roger Du-Prey's settlement with the city, are you not? You stand to be the recipient of a good deal of money, are you not?"

He turned toward Boone so rapidly and put the last of his question in such hard, rapid fire manner that Boone shrank back from him.

"Didn't you just get a large amount of money from Roger DuPrey's estate?" the last coming so quickly Boone had no time to answer his first question.

"Yes," Boone said quietly, barely audible.

"Let the record show the witness answered in the affirmative," Gundry snapped, walking away from Boone.

Stacy rose, but the judge pointed the mallet toward her and Stacy remained silent, but continued standing.

"Give the witness time to answer your question, Mister Gundry. And don't even come close to harassing this witness. He's a minor. Treat him as such."

"Yes, your honor."

To Boone, "Let's continue to look at this so called inheritance from this Roger DuPrey. It's a substantial sum, is it not?"

Boone looked at the judge who said "Mister Gundry you are a half inch away from being in contempt of this court."

"Well, your honor, I just want the record to show that

this juvenile, under age minor boy received a substantial amount of money from Roger DuPrey."

"The record will show exactly what this witness testified to. He received an amount of money from Mister DuPrey. Period. Move on to something else or this line of inquiry is over."

"Very well, your honor. Now, Boone, Miss Laster is the executor of the trust fund that was established for you from the money you received from Roger DuPrey, is she not?"

"Yes."

"And, being the executor of that trust fund, do you understand that you cannot extract any money from this trust fund without Miss Laster's approval."

"I know the conditions of the trust fund. Stacy explained them to me. She's an excellent attorney."

"Yes, yes, of course she is. So if you to want to spend any money from this fund, you would go to her and ask for permission. And, if she did not approve, you would not get the money. And, if she wanted money from the fund for whatever purpose, say maintaining the fund, expenses and stuff like that, she would not have to have your approval?"

"Objection, your honor," Stacy on her feet again. "What is this line of questioning? Boone does not know all the legal requirements of trust funds. The regulations amount to about eight legal size pages of fine print."

"Your honor, I just want to know what Boone knows about his rights and responsibilities, that's all."

"Let's leave it to Boone's attorney to advise him of that," the judge said. "Are you about through with this line of questioning?"

"Almost, your honor. Now, Boone, you are presently living in Miss Laster's house as I understand. And you lived there for some time while you had your kidnapped son with you. Did Miss Laster ever advise you to turn yourself in to the police and give the baby back to its mother?"

"I didn't take the baby from his mother. The baby's mother didn't want him, she was ashamed of him, she said. He was being adopted by some family in Iowa. The court never asked me if it was all right to give up my baby. He was my son as much as he was her son."

"Is that what your attorney, Miss Laster, advised you to do, to keep the baby because he was yours? Or did she say, you've committed a crime, you need to turn yourself in to the police and take the baby back?"

"Objections, your honor, that is privileged information, what a client's attorney advises him to do. I'm really getting a good workout jumping up and down out of my chair to object to Mister Gundry's complete and illegal line of questioning. Are we sure he is qualified to practice law in this court? May I ask for his credentials? See, your honor, I have this bad leg that doesn't bend too well thanks to the Iraqi Revolutionary Army over in Baghdad and it isn't that easy for me to rise for every amateurish question he illegally throws at my client."

"I'm getting a little tired of this myself, Mister Gundry. Did you not know that conversations between a client and their attorney are privileged information?"

"Your honor, what needs to be established here is . . ."

"Answer my question, Mister Gundry. Are you aware you can't ask for privileged information?"

"Of course, your honor, but . . ."

"Then explain why you did it and make it good."

"She's asking to be his guardian. I wanted to know if she was giving him the kind of advice a guardian should be giving him."

"It's out of bounds. Period. Move on."

"Very well. Boone, Miss Laster is an attractive woman is she not . . ."

Stacy pounded here fist on her table. "Your honor."

"Okay, let's go this way," Gundry said, "I retract that question. Now, Boone, you say you fathered a baby. To a teenage girl you were not married to, correct?"

"Yes."

"How many times did you have sex with this girl?"

Stacy was on her feet and the judge was banging her gavel as Boone was answering the question, "None of your business."

"Boone Blakely is not on trial, here,"Stacy shouted.

"Mister Gundry . . ." the judge said, but Gundry interrupted. "He's sixteen years old, your honor. Hormones are on fire inside sixteen year old boys. I'm trying to get to the real point in this hearing and that point is, why a single woman wants custody of a sixteen year old boy. Every day the news has another case of an adult female teacher enticing a teenage boy into sex. And I want to know if that's the case here. An adult woman wants a suddenly rich sixteen year old boy to leave two perfectly capable and caring parents and she invites him, and his money, to move into her bedroom."

Stacy was suddenly out of her chair, across the floor and grabbing Nelson Gundry by the lapels. "You're accusing me of sexually abusing a sixteen year old boy you ignorant low-life piece of shit."

Judge "Hard Ass Annie" Merrill smacked her bench a mighty blow with her mallet which went flying through the courtroom as the handle splintered in her hand.

27

STACY SAID, "I guess I blew it, didn't I?"

Boone agreed, nodding his head. "I was ready to come out of the chair and punch the asshole. Wish I had, you wouldn't be in trouble. What did they say to you?"

"Got a message from the Missouri Bar Association. A reprimand. I'm on suspension for 30 days."

They finished their Big Macs, sitting at the same table where Boone and Roger had met Sadie and Berkely. Stacy crumpled her napkin, propped her elbows on the table and said, "The worst part is, I won't be with you on the custody hearing for Baby John. I've got a replacement for me, Neal Howell, used to be president of the bar. He's the one helped me get admitted to the bar and probably kept me out of jail for assaulting Gundry. He's from a small town, New London, but he's been around. You can trust him."

"But it won't be you."

"You're lucky there. Hard Ass Annie has taken the case. She wasn't the original judge, but the other one was in a car accident. Hope she doesn't hold any grudges against you."

"But she didn't rule against you for custody of me, did she? I thought taking something under advisement meant the judge wanted more time to study the case. Look at case law, that sort of thing."

Stacy looked off through the grease stained window at the Red Mustang Boone had driven to the burger joint. "What I took it to mean was she was about to award me custody when I went crazy and threw old Gundry up against her bench. She could have taken that as an assault on her."

"We've got a couple of hours before I have to be in the courtroom," Boone said. "Run through what I should say again. I don't want to make a mistake."

"You did fine last time. Just speak your heart, not your head. Don't be trying to outthink the other lawyer. You'll be all right."

"What should I say when they ask me about taking Baby John. Should I admit it was wrong, that it was actually kidnapping?"

"You had a good answer to Gundry. Stick with that. He's your son. Keep saying that. The petition for custody will be from Penny, so don't be misled when she claims she wants custody. That will be necessary in order for her to have him adopted. The whole process had to go through the court again after you took him and the state had to take custody when he was taken from you. You weren't in the picture the first time. His birth certificate lists him as John Doe—there you go, his legal name is John—but you're not listed as his father and Penny is listed as an unmarried mother. You have the DNA they did on you, only the Griffins have the report. I've told Neal Howell about it so he's going to bring it up. We have proof the test was made. You actually saw the report, right. And your DNA matches Baby John's."

"Yeah, Penny showed it around at school. I didn't actually see it, but Dewey did. I gave you his name."

"Right. You prove to the court you're his father and as for the kidnapping, just stick to the line that you're his father and the mother didn't want him. You did."

Boone said, "Yeah."

Was that enough? Again, guilt rose up in him and he wondered if, in the long version of Baby John's life, would he have been better off in Iowa with another couple who probably would be loving him now every bit as much as Boone did. His thoughts jumped over to his parents. He asked Stacy, "Who do you think was paying Gundry? The senator? Penny's dad, Mister Griffin? We know it sure wasn't my parents."

"Gundry was willing to give up the senator's name so I'm guessing it came through Griffin. Probably told your dad if he wanted to keep his job, go to court for him."

"I guess it hurt them that I was there saying I didn't want to be their son anymore."

"I can understand that," Stacy said. "Now that you're a father, it's easier to understand, isn't it?"

"Yeah." Boone gathered up the debris on the table and they rose to leave. "I just wish I'd been able to get him to say Da Da."

JUDGE MERRILL took her seat at the bench with a flourish, her robe floating in the air in her wake. She tapped her brand new mallet once lightly and declared the court to be in session. The clerk laid papers in front of the judge who quickly leafed through them. She looked at Phillip Newsom who sat at the table opposite where Boone and Neal Howell sat. Newsom was middle aged, prosperous looking. The successful senior partner of a local firm. Howell was pudgy, red-faced with strong veins running through his cheeks and very little blond hair on his head. He looked completely relaxed and at ease. Boone liked that.

The judge called on Newsom. He stood to announce to the judge that this procedure had been approved already by the court, granting full custody to the mother, and this was merely a formality reiterating what had been certified previously by the court.

Neal Howell rose to inform the court that there was new information for the court that had not previously been disclosed by the petitioner in the original court proceedings. And that new information was the father, who comes now to request the court to acknowledge his rights as a parent of the subject child.

"Your honor," Newsom countered, "there has been no evidence as to the lawful father of the child."

"Because the petitioner suppressed that evidence," Howell said. "The petitioner is in possession of a DNA test that proves my client is the lawful father of the child. The petitioner has denied having such evidence, but we are prepared to call as many as ten witnesses to attest to the existence of such a test and to it's conclusions. Now, if the petitioner wants to deny under oath the existence of this material and to subject the court to the lengthy process of calling these witnesses, we are prepared to do so."

Newsom turned to confer with Frank Griffin who sat

with his wife and with Penny and Duke Mansfield. Boone wondered what Duke Mansfield was doing here.

Newsom turned back to the judge, rose and announced that his clients did not insist calling any of the potential witnesses. "They affirm the allegation by the other petitioner that he is the father and has a standing in the adjudication process here today.

Howell said, "We would insist on that proof of my client's parenting of this child be included in the record so that the question will be forever answered."

"It's a private document," Newsom said. "Requested and paid for by my client's."

"The court can accept it as such," Howell said.

Newsom looked at the Griffins, shrugged and took a document to Howell who examined it, then handed it back for Newsom to lay on the judge's bench. She looked it over and announced that it be entered into the record of this day's proceedings.

"By your petition to the court, you state that one Penny Griffin is seeking full custody of John Doe Griffin, a minor child. Is that still your request?" she asked Newsom.

"No, your honor, that has been modified to include one Duke Mansfield as a provisional parent to have custody and to properly name John Doe Griffin as Sean Elliot Mansfield. That will require a petition for a proper name change which has been introduced in court on this date."

He handed several papers to Howell and to the judge.

Boone was stunned. Custody to Duke Mansfield? How can that be? Howell was reading through the papers from Newsom and handed them to Boone. He read that Duke and

Penny were betrothed and that on the tenth of the month—eight days away—they would be married and that they request full custody on that date of Baby John and four weeks from this date his name would become Sean Elliot Mansfield. As Boone read the papers his face burned. He looked at Neal Howell and said, "No."

Howell rose to say, "Your honor, we object to the introduction of these documents of hoped-for future petitions as having no relevance to today's hearing. What we are here for today is to determine the custody of one minor child, John Doe.

Judge Merrill said, "Mister Howell is correct, Mister Newsom, this proceeding today is to determine any custody of the minor child at this time. Right now, the State of Missouri has custody. The court sees no reason for this to continue. Unless Mister Howell can cite some reason otherwise, custody will be remanded to the child's mother, as proven by the only legal document accepted by the court at this time. Mister Howell, you will have to file a separate petition with the court to have your client declared the child's father. At that time, the court will consider any changes requested in custody. Mister Newsom, your documents pertaining to a change in the child's name or in the matter of extending his custody to the mother's husband at that time is another matter to be considered separately."

Howell rose. "Your honor, the mother has acknowledged that my client is the rightful and legal father of this minor child. He is here requesting a measure of custody. I submit the court today, in these proceedings, with the evidence presented to the court by the mother can declare my client as the father and by the petition I have submitted to the court in today's matter, give a ruling on his request for custody."

Newsom said, "Your honor, we would need more time to consider this latest request of Mister Howell's.

"You received it four days ago," Howell said. "Which, I might point out, is more timely than the amendments to your petition I received five minutes ago."

Judge Merrill said, "I need some time to study this. As of now, custody of the minor child, John Doe, is awarded to his mother, Penny Griffin."

As she raised her mallet to conclude the hearing, Howell quickly said, "What about visitation rights for my client, your honor?"

With her mallet suspended in mid air, Judge Merrill said, "If your client, Mister Howell, and your client, Mister Newsom, brings to the court, not in a formal hearing, an agreement between the two for visitation, the court will consider it. If either of your clients refuse to enter into such an agreement, the court will take that into consideration in any further proceedings in this matter."

She tapped the new mallet on her bench and this time the mallet stayed intact.

"SO YOU'RE going to go see Penny about a visitation with Baby John?" Stacy asked at their dinner table.

"Yeah, guess I'll have to. I called her number and left a message on her voicemail. She lives in Columbia, with Duke Mansfield. He got a football scholarship with the university. I guess that's where they plan to live."

"You think she'll let you see him?"

"Hope so." They ate and looked across the table at each other. "I'll bet he's grown a lot."

"Yeah." They were silent as they ate. Stacy asked, "What are you prepared to give up to get to see him again?"

"What do you mean?"

"She's going to want something."

"Why do you think that?

"I've never met her, but I know something about her."

"And that is?" Boone waited, his fork in the air, motionless.

"It's about her," Stacy said. "Always has been."

28

BOONE CRUISED slowly along the streets of Eldon, drawing a stare every now and then at the red Mustang. He drove past where the Blakelys had lived, past friend Dewey's house, past the school. He had no desire to stop and talk with anyone. No one would guess that it was him, skinny, quiet Boone Blakely driving around in a forty-thousand dollar Mustang. Unless the word had gotten back to Eldon that the Blakely kid had inherited a fortune.

What would have happened in his life if he hadn't gone with Penny Griffin that night and followed the drive of aroused hormones and the charm of an attractive and sensual girl that was one of the most popular in the entire school? Where would he be? Certainly not driving such a magnificent automobile. Certainly not with a debit card in his pocket and a bank account in his name.

One event can change life forever. He felt no kinship with the town any longer. Former classmates would be clamoring over school desks and walking hallways with others their age, all in the act of growing up. Not that Boone felt any smarter now than the others, nor any older or any more grown up. But he was. All of those. And he was a father. That made all the difference in the world.

At times when he thought at length about it, it seemed to him that the sexual maturity of humans should come after life maturity is developed. That sixteen year olds should not have the capacity to propagate. Certainly he hadn't been prepared to be a parent. He was equally sure Penny wasn't. But lately, spending some quiet time by himself, waiting for Stacy to come home from the office, he realized how having and caring for Baby John had matured him. Was it scripture, the bit about when you're a child, you think as a child and when you're a man you put aside childish things? Or something like that. It had happened to him. He suddenly realized one day while giving the baby a bath that he no long thought as a child. He never thought about skateboarding, video games, BMX or motorcycles. He couldn't imagine talking today with those who had been his classmates. What would they talk about? Tests? Sports? Girls? Would the others be prepared to talk about West and Nexus and case law? About buying a house, planting a lawn and about the politics of establishing a home for veterans? About how a baby matures?

Not likely.

He drove by a warehouse he had remembered housing janitorial supplies and saw several vans and trucks parked there with Griffin Construction decals on them and remembered that Griffin had been ousted from the warehouse formerly owned by the senator. He had driven past the building some days ago where Roger had been clubbed for trespassing and seen the construction there converting it into livable quarters for veterans. Stacy was working hard to get it named the Roger DuPrey Home for Veterans.

He turned and speeded up leaving the small town

quickly. For the last time. He felt no remorse.

He no longer thought as the child who had once lived there.

PENNY LOOKED good. She always did. She smiled sweetly as she held the door open for Boone. He said hello with his own smile. He said she had a nice apartment and she said thanks. She invited him in, offered a chair, asked about a cold drink which he declined, then wished he hadn't. Duke apparently wasn't home which made Boone glad. He's been apprehensive about meeting and talking with both of them together.

"How's Baby John?" he asked after he was seated. Penny sat primly across from him. She seemed more mature to him, the way he felt about himself. Having children does that to everyone he decided.

"The woman at the state office is still keeping him. We have to make some arrangements in the apartment for him."

"He's quite a boy. I'll bet he has grown a lot since he was with me."

She nodded.

"I guess we're supposed to come up with some arrangement for my visitations. I'm anxious to see him. I've missed him."

"I imagine."

Boone wasn't finding it easy to talk with her. He wished he had brought Stacy with him, but bringing a lawyer into it probably would have delayed things. He had already decided that if Penny had a lawyer at their meeting he would immediately call Stacy. He knew he couldn't deal with another attorney without her help.

"I would like to keep him for, say, weekends. Or, if you're going to school in the daytime, maybe I could keep him while you're at school. Save you a bundle of money."

"I hear you're rich," she said.

"Where did you hear that?"

"Word gets around."

"I hear you're getting married in a couple of days."

"We've delayed that somewhat."

"You're still living with Duke?"

"He's here, off and on. Football takes up *so* much of his time."

"What does Duke think about you keeping the baby?"

Penny was looking at him like she was studying him, trying to figure something out. Boone waited while her eyes moved around on his body, concentrating on his features as if she had never seen him before.

"You screwed up my life, you know."

"You sound as if you regret that night in your car," Boone said. He tried to figure out where she was going with this. Stacy had warned him that Penny had an agenda and he had better figure out what it was.

"I could have been in the college where I wanted to go. Instead, here I am enrolled in Stephens College. For matrons. Like my mother. I'm no matron."

"You know, Penny, having a son has changed my life, too. For the better. I'm sorry you regret it so much, but I had to grow up. So I did. Maybe you should, too."

"That's insulting."

He was uncomfortable sitting here talking with her. Only the chance to see the baby again kept him from leaving.

"You didn't spend nine months carrying him around," she said, a slight tone of bitterness.

"No, I didn't. Some women find that rewarding."

Another silent spell. Then, "You're not a bad looking kid. Not as skinny and geeky as you used to be. You were pretty dumb in classes, everyone said. You look smarter now."

Boone said, "Thanks, Penny. You're as attractive as you ever were."

"You thought I was pretty hot that night, didn't you?"

"Sure."

She got out of her chair and walked around the room. From the bookcase on her wall, she took down a picture of Duke in a graduation cap and gown. She held it out so that in her vision it was side by side with Boone sitting on the sofa.

"Yeah, but old Duke has still got you beat."

He had nothing to say to that. She replaced the picture on the shelf and slowly came back to sit in the chair, folding her skirt under here legs.

"See, here's the deal. My father wants me to keep the kid out of Eldon and out of the Eldon Baptist Church where everyone can see his daughter and her bastard son. So, here I am, supposed to get married to a handsome, but immature jerk. Seems to me like everyone gets what they want except me.

"What is it you want, Penny?"

"I want to be financially independent. Not depend on daddy for things I want. I want to live like eighteen year old girls are supposed to live, like others live. To be where life is a party, someplace like Arizona State University."

"What do you think Baby John wants?"

"Someone to feed him, change his poopy diapers."

"I see," Boone said. "And that's not something you want to do."

"Anyone can do that. The lady for the state is doing it. She gets paid for it. I don't."

"Have you ever actually seen our son?"

"All babies look alike."

"When is Mrs. Allen bringing Baby John here for you to take care of?"

Penny didn't answer right away. She brushed at her hair, stood and walked around. "Tomorrow, I guess," she said. "Duke can't be here, he says. You know, *FOOTBALL*. Dear Daddy and Mother can't be here. Just me. I'm the one locked up in the prison."

"I'll come by," Boone said. "I'm anxious to see him."

Penny turned quickly, "No you won't. I don't want you here. Stay away."

Boone walked to the door, opened it, turned back to her and said, "See you tomorrow, Penny."

"DID YOU get the visitation you wanted?" Stacy asked.

"Not entirely. I'm going back tomorrow."

"So what does Penny want?"

"Money."

"How much?"

"Find out tomorrow."

"Get it in writing."

"I need you to write something up for me to make it legal. I'll get Penny to sign it and you can notarize it. Something that says I'm the father and I have all the rights of a father."

"Put something in there about visitation, just to make sure you get it. The frequency, supervised or unsupervised."

"Not necessary for this document. Maybe a separate one for the judge. I'll see how it goes tomorrow."

"Call me before you sign anything," Stacy warned.

Boone said he would. Stacy watched him, reading his face.

She said, "She's up to something. Watch out."

29

DESPITE BEING on suspension by the Bar Association, Stacy kept busy, wondering all day about Boone, Baby John and Penny. She wanted to be with them. She felt Boone needed her. He had grown into a young man these weeks he had been with her, but she still feared he would be taken advantage of by the scheming Penny.

She left work an hour earlier than usual, anxious to see how he and Penny resolved an issue so important to him. And to Stacy.

The red Mustang was not in the driveway which gave her concern. Inside, the note was the first thing she saw:

Dear Stacy,

This is not goodbye, just so long for a while. I need some time away. I'll be all right, don't worry about me. You've taught me well about life. Thanks for everything. Penny signed the paper. I gave her a check for ten thousand dollars. She said she needed money for the baby. Please see that I have enough money from the trust fund for the check to clear. I'm confident everything is going to work out for the best. I'll call you in a few days.

Love, Boone

Stacy read the note over and over. Penny needed money

for the baby. Ten thousand dollars buys a lot of diapers, she was thinking. Stacy still had the feeling Penny had taken advantage of Boone.

The house seemed very lonely that night.

THE CALL came just as she sat down to dinner. Nearly a week had passed since Boone left. Stacy had waited every night for the call. Hopefully, she said, "Hello," and waited. Boone said, "Hi, Stacy, it's me."

"Where are you?"

"I bought a house. One by the ocean like Roger always said he was going to buy."

"You bought it? Where? California? Florida?"

"I'll send you my address later. No use for you to have it right now in case my Mom and Dad should ask you where I am. Which they won't. Someone might."

"So, you need money from the trust fund? I could get into trouble over this trust fund. It has to be audited by law every year, you know."

"I just paid a down payment for right now. It's not a big house, four rooms. Kind of old, but in good shape. I got a job with a law firm here. I guess I forgot to tell you, what with everything going on, that I passed my GED test online. I'm working in the printing office of the law firm right now, but I'm taking courses to be a paralegal. The firm is helping me."

"I'm glad to hear that."

"Stacy, you took care of the money for Penny, right?"

"I did. Ten thousand dollars buys a lot of diapers, Boone.

I think Penny got to you. When do you get to visit Baby John?"

"All settled. That's what Penny said she needed, money for the baby. The law firm has an opening here for another attorney. I told them about you. They said they needed someone in house to help with veteran's cases. And my house has a sofa."

Stacy laughed. "Something to think about. Sounds like you're doing all the right things."

"I better go, Stacy. I miss being with you. There's some-one here who wants to talk with you."

"With me?"

She waited, then the baby-soft voice, "Da Da, Da Da."

THE END

www.ingramcontent.com/pod-product-compliance
Lightning Source LLC
Chambersburg PA
CBHW021035130626
46552CB00005B/1861